Dorothy Canfield Fisher

DOROTHEA FRANCES CANFIELD was born in Lawrence, Kansas, in 1879. Her mother was an artist and her father a professor of economics. She traveled extensively as a child. She received the Ph.B. from Ohio State University, studied at the Sorbonne, and received the Ph.D. in Romance languages from Columbia University.

In 1907 she married John Redwood Fisher, former captain of the Columbia football team. In the same year she inherited her great-grandfather's eighteenth-century farm in Arlington, Vermont. Fisher's love for the beautiful New England countryside prompted her to use it as the setting for many of her books.

When her husband went to Europe in 1916 to serve as an ambulance driver, the author soon followed with their two children. She spent three years in France doing war work: rehabilitating blinded French soldiers, establishing a children's convalescent home, and running a camp commissary.

After her return to Vermont, Fisher worked for the Vermont Children's Aid Society and was the first and only woman to be on the state board of education. She served as a trustee of Bennington College and Howard University and was president of the American Association of Adult Education. She continued writing well into her seventies, lectured widely, and learned foreign languages as a pastime. Eleanor Roosevelt named Fisher one of the ten most influential women in the United States.

Dorothy Canfield Fisher died in Arlington in 1958.

Understood Betsy

Dorothy Canfield Fisher

With an Afterword by Peggy Parish

Published by
Dell Publishing
a division of
Bantam Doubleday Dell Publishing Group, Inc.
1540 Broadway
New York, New York 10036

ISBN: 0-440-40796-6

RL: 6.4

Printed in the United States of America

May 1993

10 9 8 7 6 5 4 3 2

OPM

Contents

UNDERSTOOD
BETSY

Aunt Harriet
Has a Cough

When this story begins, Elizabeth Ann, who is the heroine of it, was a little girl of nine, who lived with her Great-aunt Harriet in a medium-sized city in a medium-sized state in the middle of this country; and that's all you need to know about the place, for it's not the important thing in the story; and anyhow you know all about it because it was probably very much like the place you live in yourself.

Elizabeth Ann's Great-aunt Harriet was a widow who was not very rich or very poor, and she had one daughter, Frances, who gave piano lessons to little girls. They kept a "girl" whose name was Grace and who had asthma dreadfully and wasn't very much of a "girl" at all, being nearer fifty than forty. Aunt Harriet, who was very tender-hearted, kept her chiefly because she knew that Grace could never find any other job on account of her coughing so you could hear her all over the house.

So now you know the names of all the household. And

this is how they looked: Aunt Harriet was very small and thin and old, Grace was very small and thin and middle-aged, Aunt Frances (for Elizabeth Ann called her "Aunt," although she was really, of course, a first cousin-once-removed) was small and thin and if the light wasn't too strong might be called young, and Elizabeth Ann was very small and thin and little. And yet they all had plenty to eat. I wonder what was the matter with them?

It was certainly not because they were not good, for no womenkind in all the world had kinder hearts than they. You have heard how Aunt Harriet kept Grace (in spite of the fact that she was a very depressing person) on account of her asthma; and when Elizabeth Ann's father and mother both died when she was a baby, although there were many other cousins and uncles and aunts in the family, these two women fairly rushed upon the little baby orphan, taking her home and surrounding her henceforth with the most loving devotion.

They said to themselves that it was their manifest duty to save the dear little thing from the other relatives, who had no idea about how to bring up a sensitive, impressionable child, and they were sure, from the way Elizabeth Ann looked at six months, that she was going to be a sensitive, impressionable child. It is possible also that they were a little bored with their empty life in their rather forlorn, little brick house in the medium-sized city.

But they thought that they chiefly desired to save dear Edward's child from the other kin, especially from the Putney cousins, who had written down from their Vermont farm that they would be glad to take the little girl into

their family. Aunt Harriet did not like the Vermont cousins. She used to say, "*Anything* but the Putneys!" They
were related only by marriage to her, and she had her own
opinion of them as a stiff-necked, cold-hearted, undemon-
strative, and hard set of New Englanders. "I boarded near
them one summer when you were a baby, Frances, and I
shall never forget the way they treated some children visiting there! . . . Oh, no, I don't mean they abused them or
beat them . . . but such lack of sympathy, such a starving
of the child-heart. . . . No, I shall never forget it! The
children had chores to do . . . as though they had been
hired men!"

Aunt Harriet never meant to say any of this when Elizabeth Ann could hear, but the little girl's ears were as sharp
as little girls' ears always are, and long before she was nine
she knew all about the opinion Aunt Harriet had of the
Putneys. She did not know, to be sure, what "chores" were,
but she knew from Aunt Harriet's voice that they were
something very dreadful.

There was certainly neither coldness nor hardness in the
way Aunt Harriet and Aunt Frances treated Elizabeth
Ann. They had given themselves up to the new responsibility; especially Aunt Frances, who was conscientious
about everything. As soon as the baby came there to live,
Aunt Frances stopped reading novels and magazines, and
re-read one book after another which told her how to bring
up children. She joined a Mothers' Club which met once a
week. She took a correspondence course from a school in
Chicago which taught mother-craft by mail. So you can see
that by the time Elizabeth Ann was nine years old Aunt

Frances must have known a great deal about how to bring up children. And Elizabeth Ann got the benefit of it all.

Aunt Frances always said that she and the little girl were "simply inseparable." She shared in all Elizabeth Ann's doings. In her thoughts, too. She felt she ought to share all the little girl's thoughts, because she was determined that she would thoroughly understand Elizabeth Ann down to the bottom of her little mind. Aunt Frances (down in the bottom of her own mind) thought that her mother had never *really* understood her, and she meant to do better by Elizabeth Ann. She also loved the little girl with all her heart, and longed, above everything in the world, to protect her from all harm and to keep her happy and strong and well.

Yet Elizabeth Ann was neither very strong nor well. As to her being happy, you can judge for yourself when you have read this story. She was small for her age, with a rather pale face and big dark eyes which had in them a frightened, wistful expression that went to Aunt Frances's tender heart and made her ache to take care of Elizabeth Ann better and better. Aunt Frances was afraid of a great many things herself, and she knew how to sympathize with timidity. She was always quick to reassure the little girl with all her might and main whenever there was anything to fear. When they were out walking (Aunt Frances took her out for a walk up one block and down another, every single day, no matter how tired the music lessons had made her), the aunt's eyes were always on the alert to avoid anything which might frighten Elizabeth Ann. If a big dog trotted by, Aunt Frances always said, hastily: "There,

there, dear! That's a *nice* doggie, I'm sure. I don't believe
he ever bites little girls. . . . *Mercy!* Elizabeth Ann, don't
go near him! . . . Here, darling, just get on the other side
of Aunt Frances if he scares you so" (by that time Elizabeth
Ann was always pretty well scared), "perhaps we'd better
just turn this corner and walk in the other direction." If by
any chance the dog went in that direction, too, Aunt Frances became a prodigy of valiant protection, putting the
shivering little girl behind her, threatening the animal
with her umbrella, and saying in a trembling voice, "Go
away, sir! Go *away!*"

Or if it thundered and lightninged, Aunt Frances always
dropped everything she might be doing and held Elizabeth
Ann tightly in her arms until it was all over. And at night
—Elizabeth Ann did not sleep very well—when the little
girl woke up screaming with a bad dream, it was always
dear Aunt Frances who came to her bedside, a warm wrapper over her nightgown so that she need not hurry back to
her own room, a candle lighting up her tired, kind face.
She took the little girl into her thin arms and held her
close against her thin breast. "*Tell* Aunt Frances all about
your naughty dream, darling," she would murmur, "so's to
get it off your mind!"

She had read in her books that you can tell a great deal
about children's inner lives by analyzing their dreams, and
besides, if she did not urge Elizabeth Ann to tell it, she was
afraid the sensitive, nervous little thing would "lie awake
and brood over it." This was the phrase she always used the
next day to her mother when Aunt Harriet exclaimed
about her paleness and the dark rings under her eyes. So

she listened patiently while the little girl told her all about
the fearful dreams she had, the great dogs with huge red
mouths that ran after her, the Indians who scalped her, her
schoolhouse on fire so that she had to jump from a third-
story window and was all broken to bits—once in a while
Elizabeth Ann got so interested in all this that she went on
and made up more awful things even than she had
dreamed, and told long stories which showed her to be a
child of great imagination. These dreams and continua-
tions of dreams Aunt Frances wrote down the first thing
the next morning, and tried her best to puzzle out from
them exactly what kind of little girl Elizabeth Ann was.

There was one dream, however, that even conscientious
Aunt Frances never tried to analyze, because it was too sad.
Elizabeth Ann dreamed sometimes that she was dead and
lay in a little white coffin with white roses over her. Oh,
that made Aunt Frances cry, and so did Elizabeth Ann. It
was very touching. Then, after a long, long time of talk and
tears and sobs and hugs, the little girl would begin to get
drowsy, and Aunt Frances would rock her to sleep in her
arms, and lay her down ever so quietly, and slip away to try
to get a little nap herself before it was time to get up.

At a quarter of nine every week-day morning Aunt
Frances dropped whatever else she was doing, took Elizabeth Ann's little, thin hand protectingly in hers, and led
her through the busy streets to the big brick school building where the little girl had always gone to school. It was
four stories high, and when all the classes were in session
there were six hundred children under that one roof. You
can imagine, perhaps, the noise there was on the play-

ground just before school! Elizabeth Ann shrank from it with all her soul, and clung more tightly than ever to Aunt Frances's hand as she was led along through the crowded, shrieking masses of children. Oh, how glad she was that she had Aunt Frances there to take care of her, though as a matter of fact nobody noticed the little thin girl at all, and her own classmates would hardly have known whether she came to school or not. Aunt Frances took her safely through the ordeal of the playground, then up the long, broad stairs, and pigeon-holed her carefully in her own schoolroom. She was in the third grade—3A, you understand, which is almost the fourth.

Then at noon Aunt Frances was waiting there, a patient, never-failing figure, to walk home with her little charge; and in the afternoon the same thing happened over again. On the way to and from school they talked about what had happened in the class. Aunt Frances believed in sympathizing with a child's life, so she always asked about every little thing, and remembered to inquire about the continuation of every episode, and sympathized with all her heart over the failure in mental arithmetic, and triumphed over Elizabeth Ann's beating the Schmidt girl in spelling, and was indignant over the teacher's having pets. Sometimes in telling over some very dreadful failure or disappointment Elizabeth Ann would get so wrought up that she would cry. This always brought the ready tears to Aunt Frances's kind eyes, and with many soothing words and nervous, tremulous caresses she tried to make life easier for poor little Elizabeth Ann. The days when they had cried neither of them could eat much luncheon.

After school and on Saturdays there was always the daily walk, and there were lessons, all kinds of lessons—piano lessons of course, and nature-study lessons out of an excellent book Aunt Frances had bought, and painting lessons, and sewing lessons, and even a little French, although Aunt Frances was not very sure about her pronunciation. She wanted to give the little girl every possible advantage, you see. They were really inseparable. Elizabeth Ann once said to some ladies calling on her aunts that whenever anything happened in school, the first thing she thought of was what Aunt Frances would think of it.

"Why is that?" they asked, looking at Aunt Frances, who was blushing with pleasure.

"Oh, she is so interested in my school work! And she *understands* me!" said Elizabeth Ann, repeating the phrases she had heard so often.

Aunt Frances's eyes filled with happy tears. She called Elizabeth Ann to her and kissed her and gave her as big a hug as her thin arms could manage. Elizabeth Ann was growing tall very fast. One of the visiting ladies said that before long she would be as big as her auntie, and a troublesome young lady. Aunt Frances said: "I have had her from the time she was a little baby and there has scarcely been an hour she has been out of my sight. I'll always have her confidence. You'll always tell Aunt Frances *everything*, won't you, darling?" Elizabeth Ann resolved to do this always, even if, as now, she sometimes didn't have much to tell and had to invent something.

Aunt Frances went on, to the callers: "But I do wish she weren't so thin and pale and nervous. I suppose the exciting modern life is bad for children. I try to see that she has plenty of fresh air. I go out with her for a walk every single day. But we have taken all the walks around here so often that we're rather tired of them. It's often hard to know how to get her out enough. I think I'll have to get the doctor to come and see her and perhaps give her a tonic." To Elizabeth Ann she added, hastily: "Now don't go getting notions in your head, darling. Aunt Frances doesn't think there's anything *very* much the matter with you. You'll be all right again soon if you just take the doctor's medicine nicely. Aunt Frances will take care of her precious little girl. *She*'ll make the bad sickness go away." Elizabeth Ann, who had not known that she was sick, had a picture of herself lying in the little white coffin, all covered over with white. . . . In a few minutes Aunt Frances was obliged to excuse herself from her callers and devote herself entirely to taking care of Elizabeth Ann.

One day, after this had happened several times, Aunt Frances really did send for the doctor. He came briskly in, just as Elizabeth Ann had always seen him, with his little square black bag smelling of leather, his sharp eyes, and the air of bored impatience which he always wore in that house. Elizabeth Ann was terribly afraid to see him, for she felt in her bones he would say she had galloping consumption and would die before the leaves cast a shadow. This was a phrase she had picked up from Grace, whose conversation, perhaps on account of her asthma, was full of references to early graves and quick declines.

And yet—did you ever hear of such a case before?— although Elizabeth Ann when she first stood up before the doctor had been quaking with fear lest he discover some deadly disease in her, she was very much hurt indeed when, after thumping her and looking at her lower eyelid inside out, and listening to her breathing, he pushed her away with a little jerk and said: "There's nothing in the world the matter with that child. She's as sound as a nut! What she needs is . . ."—he looked for a moment at Aunt Frances's thin, anxious face, with the eyebrows drawn together in a knot of conscientiousness, and then he looked at Aunt Harriet's thin, anxious face with the eyebrows drawn up that very same way, and then he glanced at Grace's thin, anxious face peering from the door waiting for his verdict —and then he drew a long breath, shut his lips and his little black case tightly, and did not go on to say what it was that Elizabeth Ann needed.

Of course Aunt Frances didn't let him off as easily as that. She fluttered around him as he tried to go, and she said all sorts of fluttery things to him, like, "But Doctor, she hasn't gained a pound in three months . . . and her sleep . . . and her appetite . . . and her nerves . . ."

As he put on his hat the doctor said back to her all the things doctors say under such conditions: "More beefsteak . . . plenty of fresh air . . . more sleep . . . *she*'ll be all right . . ." but his voice did not sound as though he thought what he was saying amounted to much. Nor did Elizabeth Ann. She had hoped for some spectacular red pills to be taken every half hour, like those Grace's doctor gave her whenever she felt low in her mind.

And then something happened which changed Elizabeth Ann's life forever and ever. It was a very small thing, too.

Aunt Harriet coughed. Elizabeth Ann did not think it at all a bad-sounding cough in comparison with Grace's hollow whoop; Aunt Harriet had been coughing like that ever since the cold weather set in, for three or four months now, and nobody had thought anything of it, because they were all so much occupied in taking care of the sensitive, nervous little girl.

Yet, at the sound of that small discreet cough behind Aunt Harriet's hand, the doctor whirled around and fixed his sharp eyes on her. All the bored, impatient look was gone. It was the first time Elizabeth Ann had ever seen him look interested. "What's that? What's that?" he said, going over quickly to Aunt Harriet. He snatched out of his little bag a shiny thing with two rubber tubes attached, and he put the ends of the tubes in his ears and the shiny thing up against Aunt Harriet, who was saying, "It's nothing, Doctor . . . a teasing cough I've had this winter. I meant to tell you, but I forgot it, that that sore spot on my lungs doesn't go away as it ought to."

The doctor motioned her very impolitely to stop talking, and listened hard through his little tubes. Then he turned around and looked at Aunt Frances as though he were angry at her. He said, "Take the child away and then come back here yourself."

That was almost all that Elizabeth Ann ever knew of the forces which swept her away from the life which had always gone on, revolving about her small person, exactly the same ever since she could remember.

*   *   *

You have heard so much about tears in the account of Elizabeth Ann's life so far that I won't tell you much about the few days which followed, as the family talked over and hurriedly prepared to do what the doctor said they must. Aunt Harriet was very, very sick, he told them, and must go away at once to a warm climate. Aunt Frances must go, too, but not Elizabeth Ann, for Aunt Frances would need to give all her time to taking care of Aunt Harriet. Anyhow the doctor didn't think it best, either for Aunt Harriet or for Elizabeth Ann, to have them in the same house.

Grace couldn't go, of course, but to everybody's surprise she said she didn't mind, because she had a bachelor brother, who kept a grocery store, who had been wanting her for years to go and keep house for him. She said she had stayed on just out of conscientiousness because she knew Aunt Harriet couldn't get along without her! If you notice, that's the way things often happen to very conscientious people.

Elizabeth Ann, however, had no grocer brother. She had, it is true, a great many relatives. It was settled she should go to some of them till Aunt Frances could take her back. For the time being, just now, while everything was so distracted and confused, she was to go to stay with the Lathrop cousins, who lived in the same city, although it was very evident that the Lathrops were not perfectly crazy with delight over the prospect.

Still, something had to be done at once, and Aunt Frances was so frantic with the packing up, and the moving men coming to take the furniture to storage, and her anxiety over her mother—she had switched to Aunt Harriet, you see, all the conscientiousness she had lavished on Eliz-abeth Ann—nothing much could be extracted from her about Elizabeth Ann. "Just keep her for the present, Molly!" she said to Cousin Molly Lathrop. "I'll do some-thing soon. I'll write you. I'll make another arrangement . . . but just *now* . . ."

Her voice was quavering on the edge of tears, and Cousin Molly Lathrop, who hated scenes, said hastily, "Yes, oh, yes, of course. For the present . . ." and went away, thinking that she didn't see why she should have *all* the disagreeable things to do. When she had her husband's tyrannical old mother to take care of, wasn't that enough, without adding to the household such a nervous, spoiled young one as Elizabeth Ann!

Elizabeth Ann did not, of course, for a moment dream that Cousin Molly was thinking any such things about her, but she could not help seeing that Cousin Molly was not any too enthusiastic about taking her in; and she was al-ready feeling terribly forlorn about the sudden, unexpected change in Aunt Frances, who had been *so* wrapped up in her and now was just as much wrapped up in Aunt Harriet. Do you know, I am sorry for Elizabeth Ann, and, what's more, I have been ever since this story began.

Well, since I promised you that I was not going to tell about more tears, I won't say a single word about the day when the two aunts went away on the train, for there is nothing much but tears to tell about, except perhaps an absent look in Aunt Frances's eyes which hurt the little girl's feelings dreadfully.

Then Cousin Molly took the hand of the sobbing little

girl and led her back to the Lathrop house. But if you think you are now going to hear about the Lathrops, you are quite mistaken, for just at this moment old Mrs. Lathrop took a hand in the matter. She was Cousin Molly's husband's mother, and, of course, no relation at all to Elizabeth Ann, and so was less enthusiastic than anybody else. All that Elizabeth Ann ever saw of this old lady, who now turned the current of her life again, was her head, sticking out of a second-story window; and that's all that you need to know about her, either. It was a very much agitated old head, and it bobbed and shook with the intensity with which the old voice called upon Cousin Molly and Elizabeth Ann to stop right there where they were on the front walk.

"The doctor says that what's the matter with Bridget is scarlet fever, and we've all got to be quarantined. There's no earthly sense bringing that child in to be sick and have it, and be nursed, and make the quarantine twice as long!"

"But, Mother!" called Cousin Molly. "I can't leave the child in the middle of the street!"

Elizabeth Ann was actually glad to hear her say that, because she was feeling so awfully unwanted, which is, if you think of it, not a very cheerful feeling for a little girl who has been the hub 'round which a whole household was revolving.

"You don't *have* to!" shouted old Mrs. Lathrop out of her second-story window. Although she did not add "You gump!" aloud, you could feel she was meaning just that. "You don't have to! You can just send her to the Putney cousins. All nonsense about her not going there in the first place. They invited her the minute they heard of Harriet's being so bad. They're the natural ones to take her in. Abigail is her mother's own aunt, and Ann is her own first cousin-once-removed . . . just as close as Harriet and Frances are, and *much* closer than you! And on a farm and all . . . just the place for her!"

"But how under the sun, Mother," shouted Cousin Molly back, "can I *get* her to the Putneys'? You can't send a child of nine a thousand miles without . . ."

Old Mrs. Lathrop looked again as though she were saying "You gump!" and said aloud, "Why, there's James going to New York on business in a few days anyhow. He can just go now, and take her along and put her on the right train at Albany. If he wires from here, they'll meet her in Hillsboro."

And that was just what happened. Perhaps you may have guessed by this time that people usually did what old Mrs. Lathrop told them to. As to who the Bridget was who had the scarlet fever, I know no more than you. Maybe she was the cook. Unless, indeed, old Mrs. Lathrop made her up for the occasion, which I think she would have been quite capable of doing, don't you?

At any rate, with no more ifs or ands, Elizabeth Ann's satchel was packed, and Cousin James Lathrop's satchel was packed, and the two set off together, the big, portly, middle-aged man quite as much afraid of his mother as Elizabeth Ann was. But he was going to New York, and it is conceivable that he thought once or twice on the trip that there were good times in New York as well as business engagements, whereas poor Elizabeth Ann was being sent straight to the one place in the world where there were no good times at all. Aunt Harriet had said so, ever so many times. Poor Elizabeth Ann!

Betsy Holds
the Reins

You can imagine, perhaps, the terror of Elizabeth Ann as the train carried her along toward Vermont and the horrible Putney Farm! It had happened so quickly—her satchel packed, the telegram sent, the train caught—that she had not had time to get her wits together, assert herself, and say that she would *not* go there! Besides, she had a sinking notion that perhaps they wouldn't pay any attention to her if she did. The world had come to an end now that Aunt Frances wasn't there to take care of her! Even in the most familiar air she could only half breathe without Aunt Frances! And now she was not even being taken to the Putney Farm! She was being sent!

She shrank in her seat, more and more frightened as the end of her journey came nearer, and looked out dismally at the winter landscape, thinking it hideous with its brown bare fields, its brown bare trees, and the quick-running little streams hurrying along, swollen with the January thaw

which had taken all the snow from the hills. She had heard
her elders say about her so many times that she could not
stand the cold, that she shivered at the very thought of
cold weather, and certainly nothing could look colder than
that bleak country into which the train was now slowly
making its way.

The engine puffed and puffed with great laboring breaths
that shook Elizabeth Ann's diaphragm up and down, but
the train moved more and more slowly. Elizabeth Ann
could feel under her feet how the floor of the car was
tipped up as it crept along the steep incline. "Pretty stiff
grade here?" said a passenger to the conductor.

"You bet!" he assented. "But Hillsboro is the next station and that's at the top of the hill. We go down after that
to Rutland." He turned to Elizabeth Ann—"Say, little girl,
didn't your uncle say you were to get off at Hillsboro? You'd
better be getting your things together."

Poor Elizabeth Ann's knees knocked against each other
with fear of the strange faces she was to encounter, and
when the conductor came to help her get off, he had to
carry the white, trembling child as well as her satchel. But
there was only one strange face there—not another soul in
sight at the little wooden station. A grim-faced old man in
a fur cap and heavy coat stood by a lumber wagon.

"This is her, Mr. Putney," said the conductor, touching
his cap, and went back to the train, which went away
shrieking for a nearby crossing and setting the echoes ringing from one mountain to another.

There was Elizabeth Ann alone with her much-feared
Great-uncle Henry. He nodded to her, and drew out from

the bottom of the wagon a warm, large cape, which he slipped over her shoulders. "The women folks were afraid you'd git cold drivin'," he explained. He then lifted her high to the seat, tossed her satchel into the wagon, climbed up himself, and clucked to his horses. Elizabeth Ann had always before thought it an essential part of railway journeys to be much kissed at the end and asked a great many times how you had "stood the trip."

She sat very still on the high lumber seat, feeling very forlorn and neglected. Her feet dangled high above the floor of the wagon. She felt herself to be in the most dangerous place she had ever dreamed of in her worst dreams. Oh, why wasn't Aunt Frances there to take care of her! It was just like one of her bad dreams—yes, it was horrible! She would fall, she would roll under the wheels and be crushed to . . . She looked up at Uncle Henry with the wild eyes of nervous terror which always brought Aunt Frances to her in a rush to "hear all about it," to sympathize, to reassure.

Uncle Henry looked down at her soberly, his hard, weather-beaten old face unmoved. "Here, you drive, will you, for a piece?" he said briefly, putting the reins into her hands, hooking his spectacles over his ears, and drawing out a stubby pencil and a bit of paper. "I've got some figgering to do. You pull on the left-hand rein to make 'em go to the left and t'other way for t'other way, though 'tain't likely we'll meet any teams."

Elizabeth Ann had been so near one of her wild screams of terror that now, in spite of her instant absorbed interest in the reins, she gave a queer little yelp. She was all ready with the explanation, her conversations with Aunt Frances having made her very fluent in explanations of her own emotions. She would tell Uncle Henry about how scared she had been, and how she had just been about to scream and couldn't keep back that one little . . . But Uncle Henry seemed not to have heard her little howl, or, if he had, didn't think it worth conversation, for he . . . oh, the horses were *certainly* going to one side! She hastily decided which was her right hand (she had never been forced to know it so quickly before) and pulled on that rein. The horses turned their hanging heads a little, and, miraculously, there they were in the middle of the road again.

Elizabeth Ann drew a long breath of relief and pride, and looked to Uncle Henry for praise. But he was busily setting down figures as though he were getting his 'rithmetic lesson for the next day and had not noticed . . . Oh, there they were going to the left again! This time, in her flurry, she made a mistake about which hand was which and pulled wildly on the left line! The horses docilely walked off the road into a shallow ditch, the wagon tilted . . . help! Why didn't Uncle Henry help! Uncle Henry continued intently figuring on the back of his envelope.

Elizabeth Ann, the perspiration starting out on her forehead, pulled on the other line. The horses turned back up the little slope, the wheel grated sickeningly against the wagon-box—she was *sure* they would tip over! But there! somehow there they were in the road, safe and sound, with Uncle Henry adding up a column of figures. If he only knew, thought the little girl, if he only *knew* the danger he had been in, and how he had been saved! . . . But she must think of some way to remember, for sure, which her right hand was, and avoid that hideous mistake again.

And then suddenly something inside Elizabeth Ann's head stirred and moved. It came to her, like a clap, that she needn't know which was right or left. If she just pulled the way she wanted them to go—the horses would never know whether it was the right or the left rein!

It is possible that what stirred inside her head at that moment was her brain, waking up. She was nine years old, and she was in the third-A grade at school, but that was the first time she had ever had a whole thought of her very own. At home, Aunt Frances had always known exactly what she was doing, and had helped her over the hard places before she even knew they were there; and at school her teachers had been carefully trained to think faster than the scholars. Somebody had always been explaining things to Elizabeth Ann so carefully that she had never found out a single thing for herself before. This was a very small discovery, but it was her own. Elizabeth Ann was as excited about it as a mother bird over the first egg that hatches.

She forgot how afraid she was of Uncle Henry, and poured out to him her discovery. "It's not right or left that matters!" she ended triumphantly; "it's which way you want to go!" Uncle Henry looked at her attentively as she talked, eyeing her sidewise over the top of one spectacle glass. When she finished—"Well, now, that's so," he admitted, and returned to his 'rithmetic.

It was a short remark, shorter than any Elizabeth Ann

had ever heard before. Aunt Frances and her teachers always explained matters at length. But it had a weighty, satisfying ring to it. The little girl felt the importance of having her statement recognized. She turned back to her driving.

The slow, heavy plow horses had stopped during her talk with Uncle Henry. They stood as still now as though their feet had grown to the road. Elizabeth Ann looked up at the old man for instructions. But he was deep in his figures. She had been taught never to interrupt people, so she sat still and waited for him to tell her what to do.

But, although they were driving in the midst of a winter thaw, it was a pretty cold day, with an icy wind blowing down the back of her neck. The early winter twilight was beginning to fall, and she felt rather empty. She grew tired of waiting, and remembered how the grocer's boy at home had started his horse. Then, summoning all her courage, with an uneasy glance at Uncle Henry's arithmetical silence, she slapped the reins up and down on the horses' backs and made the best imitation she could of the grocer's boy's cluck. The horses lifted their heads, they leaned forward, they put one foot before the other . . . they were off! The color rose hot on Elizabeth Ann's happy face. If she had started a big red automobile she would not have been prouder. For it was the first thing she had ever done all herself . . . every bit . . . every smitch! She had thought of it and she had done it. And it had worked!

Now for what seemed to her a long, long time she drove, drove so hard she could think of nothing else. She guided the horses around stones, she cheered them through freezing mud puddles of melted snow, she kept them in the anxiously exact middle of the road. She was quite astonished when Uncle Henry put his pencil and paper away, took the reins from her hands, and drove into a yard, on one side of which was a little low white house and on the other a big red barn. He did not say a word, but she guessed that this was Putney Farm.

Two women in gingham dresses and white aprons came out of the house. One was old and one might be called young, just like Aunt Harriet and Aunt Frances. But they looked very different from those aunts. The dark-haired one was very tall and strong-looking, and the white-haired one was very rosy and fat. They both looked up at the little, thin, white-faced girl on the high seat, and smiled. "Well, Father, you got her, I see," said the brown-haired one. She stepped up to the wagon and held up her arms to the child. "Come on, Betsy, and get some supper," she said, as though Elizabeth Ann had lived there all her life and had just driven into town and back.

And that was the arrival of Elizabeth Ann at Putney Farm.

The brown-haired one took a long, strong step or two and swung her up on the porch. "You take her in, Mother," she said. "I'll help Father unhitch."

The fat, rosy, white-haired one took Elizabeth Ann's skinny, cold little hand in her soft, warm fat one, and led her along to the open kitchen door. "I'm your Aunt Abigail," she said. "Your mother's aunt, you know. And that's your Cousin Ann that lifted you down, and it was your Uncle Henry that brought you out from town." She shut the door and went on, "I don't know if your Aunt Harriet ever happened to tell you about us, and so . . ."

Elizabeth Ann interrupted her hastily, the recollection of all Aunt Harriet's remarks vividly before her. "Oh, yes, oh, yes!" she said. "She always talked about you. She talked about you a lot, she . . ." The little girl stopped short and bit her lip.

If Aunt Abigail guessed from the expression on Elizabeth Ann's face what kind of talking Aunt Harriet's had been, she showed it only by a deepening of the wrinkles all around her eyes. She said, gravely: "Well, that's a good thing. You know all about us then." She turned to the stove and took out of the oven a pan of hot baked beans, very brown and crispy on top (Elizabeth Ann detested beans), and said, over her shoulder, "Take your things off, Betsy, and hang 'em on that lowest hook back of the door. That's *your* hook."

The little girl fumbled forlornly with the fastenings of her cape and the buttons of her coat. At home, Aunt Frances or Grace had always taken off her wraps and put them away for her. When, very sorry for herself, she turned away from the hook, Aunt Abigail said: "Now you must be cold. Pull a chair right up here by the stove." She was stepping around quickly as she put supper on the table. The floor shook under her. She was one of the fattest people Elizabeth Ann had ever seen. After living with Aunt Frances and Aunt Harriet and Grace the little girl could scarcely believe her eyes. She stared and stared.

Aunt Abigail seemed not to notice this. Indeed, she seemed for the moment to have forgotten all about the

newcomer. Elizabeth Ann sat on the wooden chair, her
feet hanging (she had been taught that it was not manners
to put her feet on the rungs), looking about her with miserable, homesick eyes. What an ugly, low-ceilinged room,
with only a couple of horrid kerosene lamps for light; and
they didn't keep any girl, evidently; and they were going to
eat right in the kitchen like poor people; and nobody spoke
to her or looked at her or asked her how she had "stood the
trip"; and here she was, millions of miles away from Aunt
Frances, without anybody to take care of her. She began to
feel the tight place in her throat which, by thinking about
hard, she could always turn into tears, and presently her
eyes began to water.

Aunt Abigail was not looking at her at all, but she now
stopped short in one of her rushes to the table, set down
the butter plate she was carrying, and said "There!" as
though she had forgotten something. She stooped—it was
perfectly amazing how spry she was—and pulled out from
under the stove a half-grown kitten, very sleepy, yawning
and stretching, and blinking its eyes. "There, Betsy!" said
Aunt Abigail, putting the little yellow and white ball into
the child's lap. "There is one of old Whitey's kittens that
didn't get given away last summer, and she pesters the life
out of me. I've got so much to do. When I heard you were
coming, I thought maybe you would take care of her for
me. If you want to, enough to bother to feed her and all,
you can have her for your own."

Elizabeth Ann bent her thin face over the warm, furry,
friendly little animal. She could not speak. She had always
wanted a kitten, but Aunt Frances and Aunt Harriet and

Grace had always been sure that cats brought diphtheria and tonsillitis and all sorts of dreadful diseases to delicate little girls. She was afraid to move for fear the little thing would jump down and run away, but as she bent cautiously toward it the necktie of her middy blouse fell forward and the kitten in the middle of a yawn struck swiftly at it with a soft paw. Then, still too sleepy to play, it turned its head and began to lick Elizabeth Ann's hand with a rough little tongue. Perhaps you can imagine how thrilled the little girl was at this! She held her hand perfectly still until the kitten stopped and began suddenly washing its own face, and then she put her hands under it and very awkwardly lifted it up, burying her face in the soft fur. The kitten yawned again, and from the pink-lined mouth came a fresh, milky breath. "Oh!" said Elizabeth Ann under her breath. "Oh, you *darling!*" The kitten looked at her with bored, speculative eyes.

Elizabeth Ann looked up now at Aunt Abigail and said, "What is its name, please?" But the old woman was busy turning over a griddle full of pancakes and did not hear. On the train Elizabeth Ann had resolved not to call these hateful relatives by the same name she had for dear Aunt Frances, but she now forgot that resolution and said, again, "Oh, Aunt Abigail, what is its name?"

Aunt Abigail faced her blankly. "Name?" she asked. "Whose . . . oh, the kitten's? Goodness, child, I stopped racking my brain for kitten names sixty years ago. Name it yourself. It's yours."

Elizabeth Ann had already named it in her own mind, the name she had always thought she *would* call a kitten by, if she ever had one. It was Eleanor, the prettiest name she knew.

Aunt Abigail pushed a pitcher toward her. "There's the cat's saucer under the sink. Don't you want to give it some milk?"

Elizabeth Ann got down from her chair, poured some milk into the saucer, and called: "Here, Eleanor! Here, Eleanor!"

Aunt Abigail looked at her sharply out of the corner of her eye and her lips twitched, but her face was quite serious as a moment later she carried the last plate of pancakes to the table.

Elizabeth Ann sat on her heels for a long time, watching the kitten lap the milk, and she was surprised, when she stood up, to see that Cousin Ann and Uncle Henry had come in, very red-cheeked from the cold air.

"Well, folks," said Aunt Abigail, "don't you think we've done some lively stepping around, Betsy and I, to get supper all on the table for you?"

Elizabeth Ann stared. What did Aunt Abigail mean? She hadn't done a thing about getting supper! But nobody made any comment, and they all took their seats and began to eat. Elizabeth Ann was astonishingly hungry, and she thought she could never get enough of the creamed potatoes, cold ham, hot cocoa, and pancakes. She was very much relieved that her refusal of beans caused no comment. Aunt Frances had always tried very hard to make her eat beans because they have so much protein in them, and growing children need protein. Elizabeth Ann had heard this said so many times she could have repeated it back-

ward, but it had never made her hate beans any the less.
However, nobody here seemed to know this, and Elizabeth
Ann kept her knowledge to herself. They had also evidently never heard how delicate her digestion was, for she
never saw anything like the number of pancakes they let
her eat. *All she wanted!* She˙ had never heard of such a
thing!

They still did not ask her how she had "stood the trip."
They did not indeed ask her much of anything or pay very
much attention to her beyond filling her plate as fast as she
emptied it. In the middle of the meal Eleanor came,
jumped into her lap, and curled down, purring. After this
Elizabeth Ann kept one hand on the little soft ball, han-
dling her fork with the other.

After supper—well, Elizabeth Ann never knew what did
happen after supper until she felt somebody lifting her and
carrying her upstairs. It was Cousin Ann, who carried her
as lightly as though she were a baby, and who said, as she
set her down on the floor in a slant-ceilinged bedroom,
"You went right to sleep with your head on the table. I
guess you're pretty tired."

Aunt Abigail was sitting on the edge of a great wide bed
with four posts, and a curtain around the top. She was
partly undressed, and was undoing her hair and brushing it
out. It was very curly and all fluffed out in a shining white
fuzz around her fat, pink face, full of soft wrinkles; but in a
moment she was braiding it up again and putting on a tight
white nightcap, which she tied under her chin.

"We got the word about your coming so late," said
Cousin Ann, "that we didn't have time to fix you up a

bedroom that can be warmed. So you're going to sleep in here for a while. The bed's big enough for two, I guess, even if they are as big as you and Mother."

Elizabeth Ann stared again. What queer things they said here. She wasn't *nearly* as big as Aunt Abigail!

"Mother, did you put Shep out?" asked Cousin Ann; and when Aunt Abigail said, "No! There! I forgot to!" Cousin Ann went away; and that was the last of *her*. They certainly believed in being saving of their words at Putney Farm.

Elizabeth Ann began to undress. She was only half awake; and that made her feel only about half her age, which wasn't very great, the whole of it, and she felt like just crooking her arm over her eyes and giving up! She was too forlorn! She had never slept with anybody before, and she had heard ever so many times how bad it was for children to sleep with grown-ups. An icy wind rattled the windows and puffed in around the loose old casings. On the window sill lay a little wreath of snow. Elizabeth Ann shivered and shook on her thin legs, undressed in a hurry, and slipped into her night dress. She felt just as cold inside as out, and never was more utterly miserable than in that strange, ugly little room with that strange, queer, fat old woman. She was even too miserable to cry, and that is saying a great deal for Elizabeth Ann!

She got into bed first, because Aunt Abigail said she was going to keep the candle lighted for a while and read. "And anyhow," she said, "I'd better sleep on the outside to keep you from rolling out."

Elizabeth Ann and Aunt Abigail lay very still for a long

time, Aunt Abigail reading out of a small, worn old book.
Elizabeth Ann could see its title, *Essays of Emerson.* A
book with that name had always laid on the center table in
Aunt Harriet's house, but that copy was all new and shiny,
and Elizabeth Ann had never seen anybody look inside it.
It was a very dull-looking book, with no pictures and no
conversation. The little girl lay on her back, looking up at
the cracks in the plaster ceiling and watching the shadows
sway and dance as the candle flickered in the gusts of cold
air. She herself began to feel a soft, pervasive warmth.
Aunt Abigail's great body was like a stove.

It was very, very quiet, quieter than any place Elizabeth
Ann had ever known, except church, because a trolley line
ran past Aunt Harriet's house and even at night there were
always more or less bangings and rattlings. Here there was
not a single sound except the soft, whispery noise when
Aunt Abigail turned over a page as she read. Elizabeth
Ann turned her head so that she could see the round, rosy
old face, full of soft wrinkles, and the calm, steady old eyes
fixed on the page. As she lay there in the warm bed, watching that quiet face, something very queer began to happen
to Elizabeth Ann. She felt as though a tight knot inside her
were slowly being untied. She felt—what was it she felt?
There are no words for it. From deep within her something
rose up softly . . . she drew one or two long, half-sobbing
breaths. . . .

Aunt Abigail laid down her book and looked over at the
child. "Do you know," she said, in a conversational tone,
"do you know, I think it's going to be real nice, having a
little girl in the house again."

Oh, then the tight knot in the little unwanted girl's heart was loosened indeed! It all gave way at once, and Elizabeth Ann burst suddenly into hot tears—yes, I know I said I would not tell you any more about her crying; but these tears were very different from any she had ever shed before. And they were the last, too, for a long, long time.

Aunt Abigail said, "Well, well!" and moving over in bed took the little weeping girl into her arms. She did not say another word then, but she put her soft, withered old cheek close against Elizabeth Ann's, 'til the sobs began to grow less, and then she said: "I hear your kitty crying outside the door. Shall I let her in? I expect she'd like to sleep with you. I guess there's room for three of us."

She got out of bed as she spoke and walked across the room to the door. The floor shook under her great bulk, and the peak of her nightcap made a long, grotesque shadow. But as she came back with the kitten in her arms, Elizabeth Ann saw nothing funny in her looks. She gave Eleanor to the little girl and got into bed again. "There, now, I guess we're ready for the night," she said. "You put the kitty on the other side of you so *she* won't fall out of bed."

She blew the light out and moved over a little closer to Elizabeth Ann, who immediately was enveloped in that delicious warmth. The kitten curled up under the little girl's chin. Between her and the terrors of the dark room loomed the rampart of Aunt Abigail's great body.

Elizabeth Ann drew a long, long breath . . . and when she opened her eyes the sun was shining in at the window.

A Short Morning

Aunt Abigail was gone, Eleanor was gone. The room was quite empty except for the bright sunshine pouring in through the small-paned windows. Elizabeth Ann stretched and yawned and looked about her. What funny wallpaper it was—so old-fashioned looking! The picture was of a blue river and a brown mill, with green willow trees over it, and a man with sacks on his horse's back stood in front of the mill. This picture was repeated a great many times, all over the paper; and in the corner, where it hadn't come out even, they had had to cut it right down the middle of the horse. It was very curious-looking. She stared at it a long time, waiting for somebody to tell her when to get up. At home Aunt Frances always told her, and helped her get dressed. But here nobody came. She discovered that the heat came from a hole in the floor near the bed, which opened down into the room below. From it came a warm breath of baking bread and a muffled thump once in a while.

The sun rose higher and higher, and Elizabeth Ann grew hungrier and hungrier. Finally it occurred to her that it was not absolutely necessary to have somebody tell her to get up. She reached for her clothes and began to dress. When she had finished she went out into the hall, and with a return of her aggrieved, abandoned feeling (you must remember that her stomach was very empty) she began to try to find her way downstairs. She soon found the steps, went down them one at a time, and pushed open the door at the foot. Cousin Ann, the brown-haired one, was ironing near the stove. She nodded and smiled as the child came into the room, and said, "Well, you must feel rested!"

"Oh, I haven't been asleep!" explained Elizabeth Ann. "I was waiting for somebody to tell me to get up."

"Oh," said Cousin Ann, opening her black eyes a little. "*Were* you?" She said no more than this, but Elizabeth Ann decided hastily that she would not add, as she had been about to, that she was also waiting for somebody to help her dress and do her hair. As a matter of fact, she had greatly enjoyed doing her own hair—the first time she had ever tried it. It had never occurred to Aunt Frances that her little baby girl had grown up enough to be her own hairdresser, nor had it occurred to Elizabeth Ann that this might be possible. But as she struggled with the snarls she had had a sudden wild idea of doing it a different way from the pretty fashion Aunt Frances always followed. Elizabeth Ann had always secretly envied a girl in her class whose hair was all tied back from her face, with one big knot in her ribbon at the back of her neck. It looked so grown-up. And this morning she had done hers that way, turning her neck till it ached, so that she could see the coveted tight effect at the back. And still—aren't little girls queer?—

although she had enjoyed doing her own hair, she was very much inclined to feel hurt because Cousin Ann had not come to do it for her.

Cousin Ann set her iron down with the soft thump which Elizabeth Ann had heard upstairs. She began folding a napkin, and said: "Now reach yourself a bowl off the shelf yonder. The oatmeal's in that kettle on the stove and the milk is in the blue pitcher. If you want a piece of bread and butter, here's a new loaf just out of the oven, and the butter's in that brown crock."

Elizabeth Ann followed these instructions and sat down before this quickly assembled breakfast in a very much surprised silence. At home it took the girl more than half an hour to get breakfast and set the table, and then she had to wait on them besides. She began to pour the milk out of the pitcher and stopped suddenly. "Oh, I'm afraid I've taken more than my share!" she said apologetically.

Cousin Ann looked up from her rapidly moving iron, and said, in an astonished voice: "Your share? What do you mean?"

"My share of the quart," explained Elizabeth Ann. At home they bought a quart of milk and a cup of cream every day, and they were all very conscientious about not taking more than their due share.

"Good land, child, take all the *milk* you want!" said Cousin Ann, as though she found something shocking in what the little girl had just said. Elizabeth Ann thought to herself that she spoke as though milk ran out of a faucet, like water.

She was fond of milk, and she made a good breakfast as

she sat looking about the low-ceilinged room. It was unlike any room she had ever seen.

It was, of course, the kitchen, and yet it didn't seem possible that the same word could be applied to that room and the small, dark cubbyhole which had been Grace's asthmatical kingdom. This room was very long and narrow, and all along one side were windows with white, ruffled curtains drawn back at the sides, and with small, shining panes of glass, through which the sun poured golden light on a long shelf of potted plants that took the place of a window sill. The shelf was covered with shining white oil cloth, the pots were of clean reddish-brown, the sturdy, stocky plants of bright green with clear red-and-white flowers. Elizabeth Ann's eyes wandered all over the kitchen from the low, white ceiling to the clean, bare wooden floor, but they always came back to those sunny windows. Once, back in the big brick school building, as she had sat drooping her thin shoulders over her desk, some sort of a procession had gone by with a brass band playing a lively air. For some reason, every time she now glanced at that sheet of sunlight and the bright flowers she had a little of the same thrill which had straightened her back and gone up and down her spine while the band was playing. Possibly Aunt Frances was right, after all, and Elizabeth Ann *was* a very impressionable child. I wonder, by the way, if anybody ever saw a child who wasn't.

At one end, the end where Cousin Ann was ironing, stood the kitchen stove, gleaming black, with a teakettle humming away on it, a big hot-water boiler near it, and a large kitchen cabinet with lots of drawers and shelves and hooks and things. Beyond that, in the middle of the room, was the table where they had had supper last night, and at which the little girl now sat eating her very late breakfast; and beyond that, at the other end of the room, was another table with an old dark-red cashmere shawl on it for a cover. A large lamp stood in the middle of this, a bookcase near it, two or three rocking chairs around it, and back of it, against the wall, was a wide sofa covered with bright cretonne, with three bright pillows. Something big and black and woolly was lying on this sofa, snoring loudly. As Cousin Ann saw the little girl's fearful glance alight on this she explained: "That's Shep, our old dog. Doesn't he make an awful noise! Mother says, when she happens to be alone here in the evening, it's real company to hear Shep snore —as good as having a man in the house."

Although this did not seem at all a sensible remark to Elizabeth Ann, who thought soberly to herself that she didn't see why snoring made a dog as good as a man, still she was acute enough (for she was really quite an intelligent little girl) to feel that it belonged in the same class of remarks as one or two others she had noted as "queer" in the talk at Putney Farm last night. This variety of talk was entirely new to her, nobody in Aunt Harriet's conscientious household ever making anything but plain statements of fact. It was one of the "queer Putney ways" which Aunt Harriet had forgotten to mention. It is possible that Aunt Harriet had never noticed it.

When Elizabeth Ann finished her breakfast, Cousin Ann made three suggestions, using exactly the same accent for them all. She said: "Hadn't you better wash your dishes

up now before they get sticky? And don't you want one of
those red apples from the dish on the side table? And then
maybe you'd like to look around the house so's to know
where you are." Elizabeth Ann had never washed a dish in
all her life, and she had always thought that nobody but
poor, ignorant people, who couldn't afford to hire girls, did
such things. And yet (it was odd) she did not feel like
saying this to Cousin Ann, who stood there so straight in
her gingham dress and apron, with her clear, bright eyes
and red cheeks. Besides this feeling, Elizabeth Ann was
overcome with embarrassment at the idea of undertaking a
new task in that casual way. How in the world *did* you wash
dishes? She stood rooted to the spot, irresolute, horribly
shy, and looking, though she did not know it, very clouded
and sullen. Cousin Ann said briskly, holding an iron up to
her cheek to see if it was hot enough: "Just take them over
to the sink there and hold them under the hot water faucet. They'll be clean in no time. The dish towels are those
hanging on the rack over the stove."

Elizabeth Ann moved promptly over to the sink, as
though Cousin Ann's words had shoved her there, and
before she knew it, her saucer, cup, and spoon were clean
and she was wiping them on a dry checked towel. "The
spoon goes in the sidetable drawer with the other silver,
and the saucer and cup in those shelves there behind the
glass doors where the china belongs," continued Cousin
Ann, thumping hard with her iron on a napkin and not
looking up at all, "and don't forget your apple as you go
out. Those Northern Spies are just getting to be good

about now. When they first come off the tree in October you could shoot them through an oak plank."

Now Elizabeth Ann knew that this was a foolish thing to say, since of course an apple never could go through a board; but something that had always been sound asleep in her brain woke up a little, little bit and opened one eye. For it occurred dimly to Elizabeth Ann that this was a rather funny way of saying that Northern Spies are very hard when you first pick them in the autumn. She had to figure it out for herself slowly, because it was a new idea to her, and she was halfway through her tour of inspection of the house before there glimmered on her lips, in a faint smile, the first recognition of a joke in all her life. She felt like calling down to Cousin Ann that she saw the point, but before she had taken a single step toward the head of the stairs she had decided not to do this. Cousin Ann, with her bright, dark eyes, and her straight back, and her long arms, and her way of speaking as though it never occurred to her that you wouldn't do just as she said—Elizabeth Ann was not sure that she liked Cousin Ann, and she was very sure that she was afraid of her.

So she went on, walking from one room to another, industriously eating the red apple, the biggest she had ever seen. It was the best, too, with its crisp, white flesh and the delicious, sour-sweet juice which made Elizabeth Ann feel with each mouthful like hurrying to take another. She did not think much more of the other rooms in the house than she had of the kitchen. There were no draped "throws" over anything; there were no lace curtains at the windows, just dotted Swiss like the kitchen; all the ceilings were very low; the furniture was all of dark wood and very old-looking; what few rugs there were were of bright-colored rags; the mirrors were queer and old, with funny pictures at the top; all the beds were old wooden ones with posts, and curtains round the tops; and there was not a single plush portière in the parlor, whereas at Aunt Harriet's there had been two sets for that one room.

She was glad to see no piano. In her heart she had not liked her music lessons at all, but she had never dreamed of not accepting them from Aunt Frances as she accepted everything else. Also she had liked to hear Aunt Frances boast about how much better she could play than other children of her age.

She was downstairs by this time, and, opening a door out of the parlor, found herself back in the kitchen, the long line of sunny windows and the bright flowers giving her that quick little thrill again. Cousin Ann looked up from her ironing, nodded, and said: "All through? You'd better come in and get warmed up. Those rooms get awfully cold these January days. Winters we mostly use this room so's to get the good of the kitchen stove." She added after a moment, during which Elizabeth Ann stood by the stove, warming her hands: "There's one place you haven't seen yet—the milk room. Mother's down there now, churning. That's the door—the middle one."

Elizabeth Ann had been wondering and wondering where in the world Aunt Abigail was. So she stepped quickly to the door, and went down the cold dark stairs she found there. At the bottom was a door, locked apparently, for she could find no fastening. She heard steps inside, the door was briskly cast open, and she almost fell into the arms of Aunt Abigail, who caught her as she stumbled forward, saying: "Well, I've been expectin' you down here for a long time. I never saw a little girl yet who didn't like to watch butter-making. Don't you love to run the butter-worker over it? I do, myself, for all I'm seventy-two!"

"I don't know anything about it," said Elizabeth Ann. "I don't know what you make butter out of. We always bought ours."

"Well, *for goodness' sakes!*" said Aunt Abigail. She turned and called across the room. "Henry, did you ever! Here's Betsy saying she doesn't know what we make butter out of! She actually never saw anybody making butter!"

Uncle Henry was sitting down, near the window, turning the handle of a small barrel swung between two uprights. He stopped for a moment and considered Aunt Abigail's remark with the same serious attention he had given to Elizabeth Ann's discovery about left and right. Then he began to turn the churn over and over again and said, peaceably: "Well, Mother, you never saw anybody laying asphalt pavement, I'll warrant you! And I suppose Betsy knows all about that."

Elizabeth Ann's spirits rose. She felt very superior indeed. "Oh, yes," she assured them, "I know *all* about that! Didn't you ever see anybody doing that? Why, I've seen them *hundreds* of times! Every day as we went to school they were doing over the whole pavement for blocks along there."

Aunt Abigail and Uncle Henry looked at her with interest, and Aunt Abigail said: "Well, now, think of that! Tell us all about it!"

"Why, there's a big black sort of wagon," began Elizabeth Ann, "and they run it up and down and pour out the black stuff on the road. And that's all there is to it." She stopped, rather abruptly, looking uneasy. Uncle Henry inquired: "Now there's one thing I've always wanted to know. How do they keep that stuff from hardening on them? How do they keep it hot?"

The little girl looked blank. "Why, a fire, I suppose," she faltered, searching her memory desperately and finding there only a dim recollection of a red glow somewhere connected with the familiar scene.

"Of course a fire," agreed Uncle Henry. "But what do they burn in it, coke or coal or wood or charcoal? And how do they get any draft to keep it going?"

Elizabeth Ann shook her head. "I never noticed," she said.

Aunt Abigail asked her now, "What do they do to the road before they pour it on?"

"Do?" said Elizabeth Ann. "I didn't know they did anything."

"Well, they can't pour it right on a dirt road, can they?" asked Aunt Abigail. "Don't they put down cracked stone or something?"

Elizabeth Ann looked down at her toes. "I never noticed," she said.

"I wonder how long it takes for it to harden?" said Uncle Henry.

"I never noticed," said Elizabeth Ann, in a small voice.

Uncle Henry said, "Oh!" and stopped asking questions. Aunt Abigail turned away and put a stick of wood in the stove. Elizabeth Ann did not feel very superior now, and when Aunt Abigail said, "Now the butter's beginning to come. Don't you want to watch and see everything I do, so's you can answer if anybody asks you how butter is made?" Elizabeth Ann understood perfectly what was in Aunt Abigail's mind, and gave to the process of butter-making a more alert and aroused attention than she had ever before given to anything. It was so interesting, too, that in no time she forgot why she was watching, and was absorbed in the fascinations of the dairy for their own sake.

She looked in the churn as Aunt Abigail unscrewed the top, and saw the thick, sour cream separating into butter-milk and tiny golden particles. "It's gathering," said Aunt Abigail, screwing the lid back on. "Father'll churn it a little more till it really comes. And you and I will scald the wooden butter things and get everything ready. You'd bet-ter take that apron there to keep your dress clean."

Wouldn't Aunt Frances have been astonished if she could have looked in on Elizabeth Ann that very first morning of her stay at the hateful Putney Farm and have seen her wrapped in a gingham apron, her face bright with interest, trotting here and there in the stone-floored milk room! She was allowed the excitement of pulling out the plug from the bottom of the churn, and dodged back hast-ily to escape the gush of buttermilk spouting into the pail held by Aunt Abigail. And she poured the water in to wash the butter, and screwed on the top herself, and, again all herself (for Uncle Henry had gone off as soon as the

butter had "come"), swung the barrel back and forth six or
seven times to swish the water all through the particles of
butter. She even helped Aunt Abigail scoop out the great
yellow lumps—her imagination had never conceived of so
much butter in all the world! Then Aunt Abigail let her
run the curiously shaped wooden butter-worker back and
forth over the butter, squeezing out the water, and then
pile it up again with her wooden paddle into a mound of
gold. She weighed out the salt needed on the scales, and
was very much surprised to find that there really is such a
thing as an ounce. She had never met it before outside the
pages of her arithmetic book and she didn't know it lived
anywhere else.

After the salt was worked in she watched Aunt Abigail's
deft, wrinkled old hands make pats and rolls. It looked like
the greatest fun, and too easy for anything; and when Aunt
Abigail asked her if she wouldn't like to make up the last
half pound into a pat for dinner, she took up the wooden
paddle confidently. And then she got one of the surprises
that Putney Farm seemed to have for her. She discovered
that her hands didn't seem to belong to her at all, that her
fingers were all thumbs, that she didn't seem to know in
the least beforehand how hard a stroke she was going to
give nor which way her fingers were going to go. It was, as
a matter of fact, the first time Elizabeth Ann tried to do
anything with her hands except to write and figure and
play on the piano, and naturally she wasn't very well ac-
quainted with them. She stopped in dismay, looking at the
shapeless, battered heap of butter before her and holding
out her hands as though they were not part of her.

Aunt Abigail laughed, took up the paddle, and after three or four passes the butter was a smooth, yellow ball. "Well, that brings it all back to me!" she said—"when *I* was a little girl, when my grandmother first let me try to make a pat. I was about five years old—my! what a mess I made of it! And I remember—doesn't it seem funny—that *she* laughed and said her Great-aunt Elmira had taught her how to handle butter right here in this very milk room. Let's see, Grandmother was born the year the Declaration of Independence was signed. That's quite a while ago, isn't it? But butter hasn't changed much, I guess, nor little girls either."

Elizabeth Ann listened to this statement with a very queer, startled expression on her face, as though she hadn't understood the words. Now for a moment she stood staring up in Aunt Abigail's face, and yet not seeing her at all, because she was thinking so hard. She was thinking! "Why! There were real people living when the Declaration of Independence was signed—real people, not just history people—old women teaching little girls how to do things —right in this very room, on this very floor—and the Declaration of Independence just signed!"

To tell the honest truth, although she had passed a very good examination in the little book on American history they had studied in school, Elizabeth Ann had never to that moment had any notion that there ever had been really and truly any Declaration of Independence at all. It had been like the ounce, living only inside her schoolbooks for little girls to be examined about. And now here Aunt Abigail, talking about a butter-pat, had brought it to life!

Of course all this only lasted a moment, because it was such a new idea! She soon lost track of what she was thinking of; she rubbed her eyes as though she were coming out of a dream, she thought, confusedly: "What did butter have to do with the Declaration of Independence? Nothing, of course! It couldn't!" and the whole impression seemed to pass out of her mind. But it was an impression which was to come again and again during the next few months.

Betsy Goes
to School

Elizabeth Ann was very much surprised to hear Cousin Ann's voice calling, "Dinner!" down the stairs. It did not seem possible that the whole morning had gone by. "Here," said Aunt Abigail, "just put that pat on a plate, will you, and take it upstairs as you go. I've got all I can do to haul my own two hundred pounds up, without any half pound of butter into the bargain." The little girl smiled at this, though she did not exactly know why, and skipped up the stairs proudly with her butter.

Dinner was smoking on the table, which was set in the midst of the great pool of sunlight. A very large black dog, with a great bushy tail, was walking around and around the table, sniffing the air. He looked as big as a bear to Elizabeth Ann; and as he walked his great red tongue hung out of his mouth and his white teeth gleamed horribly. Elizabeth Ann shrank back in terror, clutching her plate of butter to her breast with tense fingers. Cousin Ann said, over her shoulder: "Oh, bother! There's old Shep, got up to pester us begging for scraps! *Shep!* You go and lie down this minute!"

To Elizabeth Ann's astonishment and immense relief, the great animal turned, drooping his head sadly, walked back across the floor, got up on the couch again, and laid his head down on one paw very forlornly, turning up the whites of his eyes meekly at Cousin Ann.

Aunt Abigail, who had just pulled herself up the stairs, panting, said, between laughing and puffing, "I'm glad I'm not an animal on this farm. Ann does boss them around so."

"Well, *some*body has to!" said Cousin Ann, advancing on the table with a platter. This proved to have chicken fricassee on it, and Elizabeth Ann's heart melted in her at the smell. She loved chicken gravy on hot biscuits beyond anything in the world, but chickens are so expensive when you buy them in the market that Aunt Harriet hadn't had them very often for dinner. And there was a plate of biscuits, golden brown, just coming out of the oven! She sat down very quickly, her mouth watering, and attacked the big plateful of food which Cousin Ann passed her.

At Aunt Harriet's she had always been aware that everybody watched her anxiously as she ate, and she had heard so much about her light appetite that she felt she must live up to her reputation, and had a natural and human hesitation about eating all she wanted when there happened to be something she liked very much. But nobody here knew that she "only ate enough to keep a bird alive," and that her "appetite was *so* capricious!" Nor did anybody notice her while she stowed away the chicken and gravy and hot

biscuits and currant jelly and baked potatoes and apple pie
—when did Elizabeth Ann ever eat such a meal before?
She actually felt her belt grow tight.

In the middle of the meal Cousin Ann got up to answer
the telephone, which was in the next room. The instant
the door had closed behind her, Uncle Henry leaned forward, tapped Elizabeth Ann on the shoulder, and nodded
toward the sofa. His eyes were twinkling, and as for Aunt
Abigail, she began to laugh silently, shaking all over, her
napkin at her mouth to stifle the sound. Elizabeth Ann
turned wonderingly and saw the old dog cautiously and
noiselessly letting himself down from the sofa, one ear
cocked rigidly in the direction of Cousin Ann's voice in
the next room. "The old tyke!" said Uncle Henry. "He
always sneaks up to the table to be fed if Ann goes out for a
minute. Here, Betsy, you're nearest, give him this piece of
skin from the chicken neck." The big dog padded forward
across the room, evidently in such a state of terror about
Cousin Ann that Elizabeth Ann felt for him. She had a
fellow-feeling about that relative of hers. Also it was impossible to be afraid of so meek and guilty an animal. As
old Shep came up to her, poking his nose inquiringly on
her lap, she shrinkingly held out the big piece of skin, and
though she jumped back at the sudden snap and gobbling
gulp with which the old dog greeted the tidbit, she could
not but sympathize with his evident enjoyment of it. He
waved his bushy tail gratefully, cocked his head on one
side, and, his ears standing up at attention, his eyes glistening greedily, he gave a little, begging whine. "Oh, he's
asking for more!" cried Elizabeth Ann, surprised to see how

plainly she could understand dog talk. "Quick, Uncle Henry, give me another piece!"

Uncle Henry rapidly transferred to her plate a wing bone from his own, and Aunt Abigail, with one deft swoop, contributed the neck from the platter. As fast as she could, Elizabeth Ann fed these to Shep, who woofed them down at top speed, the bones crunching loudly under his strong, white teeth. It did your heart good to see how he enjoyed it!

There was the sound of the telephone receiver being hung up in the next room—and everybody acted at once. Aunt Abigail began drinking innocently out of her coffee cup, only her laughing old eyes showing over the rim; Uncle Henry buttered a slice of bread with a grave face, as though he were deep in conjectures about who would be the next President; and as for old Shep, he made one plunge across the room, his toenails clicking on the bare floor, sprang up on the couch, and when Cousin Ann opened the door and came in, he was lying in exactly the position in which she had left him, his paws stretched out, his head laid on them, his brown eyes turned up meekly so that the whites showed.

I've told you what these three did, but I haven't told you yet what Elizabeth Ann did. And it is worth telling. As Cousin Ann stepped in, glancing suspiciously from her sober-faced and abstracted parents to the lamblike innocence of old Shep, little Elizabeth Ann burst into a shout of laughter. It's worth telling about, because, so far as I know, that was the first time she had ever laughed out heartily in all her life. For my part, I'm half surprised to know that she knew how.

Of course, when she laughed, Aunt Abigail had to laugh, too, setting down her coffee cup and showing all the funny wrinkles in her face screwed up hard with fun; and that made Uncle Henry laugh, and then Cousin Ann laughed and said, as she sat down, "You are bad children, the whole four of you!" And old Shep, seeing the state of things, stopped pretending to be meek, jumped down, and came lumbering over to the table, wagging his tail and laughing too; you know, that good, wide dog smile! He put his head on Elizabeth Ann's lap again and she patted it and lifted up one of his big black ears. She had forgotten that she was terribly afraid of big dogs.

After dinner Cousin Ann looked up at the clock and said: "My goodness! Betsy'll be late for school if she doesn't start right off." She explained to the child, aghast at this sudden thunderclap, "I let you sleep this morning as long as you wanted to, because you were so tired from your journey. But of course there's no reason for missing the afternoon session."

As Elizabeth Ann continued sitting perfectly still, frozen with alarm, Cousin Ann jumped up briskly, got the little coat and cap, helped her up, and began inserting the child's arms into the sleeves. She pulled the cap well down over Elizabeth Ann's ears, felt in the pocket and pulled out the mittens. "There," she said, holding them out, "you'd better put them on before you go out, for it's a real cold day." As she led the stupefied little girl along toward the door, Aunt Abigail came after them and put a big sugar

cookie into the child's hand. "Maybe you'll like to eat that
for your recess time," she said. "I always did when I went to
school."

Elizabeth Ann's hand closed automatically about the
cookie, but she scarcely heard what was said. She felt herself to be in a bad dream. Aunt Frances had never, no
never, let her go to school alone, and on the first day of the
year always took her to the new teacher and introduced
her and told the teacher how sensitive she was and how
hard to understand; and then she stayed there for an hour
or two till Elizabeth Ann got used to things! She could not
face a whole new school all alone—oh, she couldn't, she
wouldn't! She couldn't! Horrors! Here she was in the front
hall—she was on the porch! Cousin Ann was saying: "Now
run along, child. Straight down the road till the first turn
to the left, and there in the crossroads, there you are." And
now the front door closed behind her, the path stretched
before her to the road, and the road led down the hill the
way Cousin Ann had pointed. Elizabeth Ann's feet began
to move forward and carried her down the path, although
she was still crying out to herself, "I can't! I won't! I
can't!"

Are you wondering why Elizabeth Ann didn't turn right
around, open the front door, walk in, and say, "I can't! I
won't! I can't!" to Cousin Ann?

The answer to that question is that she didn't do it because Cousin Ann was Cousin Ann. There's more in that
than you think! In fact, there is a mystery in it that nobody
has ever solved, not even the greatest scientists and philosophers, although, like all scientists and philosophers, they

think they have gone a long way toward explaining some-thing they don't understand by calling it a long name. The long name is "personality," and what it means nobody knows, but for all that, it is perhaps the very most impor-tant thing in the world. Yet we know only one or two things about it. We know that anybody's personality is made up of the sum total of all the actions and thoughts and desires of his life. And we know that though there aren't any words or any figures in any languages to set down that sum total accurately, still it is one of the first things that everybody knows about anybody else. And that really is all we know!

So I can't tell you why Elizabeth Ann did not go back and cry and sob and say she couldn't and she wouldn't and she couldn't as she would certainly have done at Aunt Harriet's. You remember that I could not even tell you why it was that, as the little fatherless and motherless girl lay in bed looking at Aunt Abigail's old face, she should feel so comforted and protected that she must needs break out crying. No, all I can say is that it was because Aunt Abigail was Aunt Abigail. But perhaps it may occur to you that it's rather a good idea to keep a sharp eye on your "personal-ity," whatever that is! It might be handy, you know, to have a personality like Cousin Ann's which sent Elizabeth Ann's feet down the path; or perhaps you would prefer one like Aunt Abigail's. Well, take your choice.

You must not, of course, think for a moment that Eliza-beth Ann had the slightest *intention* of obeying Cousin Ann. No indeed! Nothing was farther from her mind as her feet carried her along the path and into the road. In her mind was nothing but rebellion and fear and anger and oh, such hurt feelings! She turned sick at the very thought of facing all the staring, curious faces in the playground turned on the new scholar as she had seen them do at home! She would never, never do it! She would walk around all the afternoon, and then go back and tell Cousin Ann that she couldn't! She would *explain* to her how Aunt Frances never let her go out of doors without a loving hand to cling to. She would *explain* to her how Aunt Frances always took care of her! . . . It was easier to think about what she would say and do and explain, away from Cousin Ann, than it was to say and do it before those black eyes. Aunt Frances's eyes were soft, light blue.

Oh, how she wanted Aunt Frances to take care of her! Nobody cared a thing about her! Nobody *understood* her but Aunt Frances! She wouldn't go back at all to Putney Farm. She would just walk on and on till she was lost, and the night would come and she would lie down and freeze to death, and then wouldn't Cousin Ann feel . . . Someone called to her, "Isn't this Betsy?"

She looked up astonished. A young girl in a gingham dress and a white apron like those at Putney Farm stood in front of a tiny, square building, like a toy house. "Isn't this Betsy?" asked the young girl again. "Your Cousin Ann said you were coming to school today and I've been looking out for you. But I saw you going right by, and I ran out to stop you."

"Why, where *is* the school?" asked Betsy, staring around for a big brick, four-story building.

The young girl laughed and held out her hand. "This is

the school," she said, "and I am the teacher, and you'd better come right in, for it's time to begin."

She led Betsy into a low-ceilinged room with geraniums at the windows, where about a dozen children of different ages sat behind their desks. At the first sight of them Betsy blushed crimson with fright and shyness, and hung down her head; but, looking out the corners of her eyes, she saw that they, too, were all red-faced and scared-looking and hung down their heads, looking at her shyly out of the corners of their eyes. She was so surprised by this that she forgot all about herself and looked inquiringly at the teacher.

"They don't see many strangers," the teacher explained, "and they feel shy and scared when a new scholar comes, especially one from the city."

"Is this my grade?" asked Elizabeth, thinking it the very smallest grade she had ever seen.

"This is the whole school," said the teacher. "There are only two or three in each class. You'll probably have three in yours. Miss Ann said you were in the third grade. There, that's your seat."

Elizabeth sat down before a very old desk, much battered and hacked up with knife marks. There was a big H. P. carved just over the inkwell, and many other initials scattered all over the top.

The teacher stepped back to her desk and took up a violin that lay there. "Now, children, we'll begin the afternoon session by singing 'America,' " she said. She played the air over a little, sweetly and stirringly, and then as the children stood up she came down close to them, standing

just in front of Betsy. She drew the bow across the strings
in a big chord, and said, *"Now,"* and Betsy burst into song
with the others. The sun came in the windows brightly, the
teacher, too, sang as she played, and the children, even the
littlest ones, opened their mouths wide and sang with all
their hearts.

What Grade Is Betsy?

After the singing the teacher gave Elizabeth Ann a pile of schoolbooks, some paper, some pencils, and a pen, and told her to set her desk in order. There were more initials carved inside, another big H. P. with a little A. P. under it. What a lot of children must have sat there, thought the little girl as she arranged her books and papers. As she shut down the lid the teacher finished giving some instructions to three or four little ones and said, "Betsy and Ralph and Ellen, bring your reading books up here."

Betsy sighed, took out her third-grade reader, and went with the other two up to the battered old bench near the teacher's desk. She knew all about reading lessons and she hated them, although she loved to read. But reading lessons! . . . You sat with your book open at some reading that you could do with your eyes shut, it was so easy, and you waited and waited and waited while your classmates slowly stumbled along, reading aloud a sentence or two apiece, until your turn came to stand up and read your sentence or two, which by that time sounded just like nonsense because you'd read it over and over so many times to

yourself before your chance came. And often you didn't
even have a chance to do that, because the teacher didn't
have time to get around to you at all, and you closed your
book and put it back in your desk without having opened
your mouth. Reading was one thing Elizabeth Ann had
learned to do very well indeed, but she had learned it all by
herself at home from much reading to herself. Aunt Frances had kept her well supplied with children's books from
the nearest public library. She often read three a week—
very different, that, from a sentence or two once or twice a
week.

When she sat down on the battered old bench she almost laughed aloud, it seemed so funny to be in a class of
only three. There had been forty in her grade in the big
brick building. She sat in the middle, the little girl whom
the teacher had called Ellen on one side, and Ralph on the
other. Ellen was very pretty, with fair hair smoothly
braided in two little pigtails, sweet, blue eyes, and a clean
blue-and-white gingham dress. Ralph had very black eyes,
dark hair, a big bruise on his forehead, a cut on his chin,
and a tear in the knee of his short trousers. He was much
bigger than Ellen, and Elizabeth Ann thought he looked
rather fierce. She decided that she would be afraid of him,
and would not like him at all.

"Page thirty-two," said the teacher. "Ralph first."

Ralph stood up and began to read. It sounded familiar to
Elizabeth Ann, for he did not read at all well. What was
not familiar was that the teacher did not stop him after the
first sentence. He read on and on till he had read a page,
the teacher only helping him with the hardest words.

"Now Betsy," said the teacher.

Elizabeth Ann stood up, read the first sentence, and paused, like a caged lion pausing when he comes to the end of his cage.

"Go on," said the teacher.

Elizabeth Ann read the next sentence and stopped again, automatically.

"Go *on*," said the teacher, looking at her sharply.

The next time the little girl paused the teacher laughed out good-naturedly. "What is the matter with you, Betsy?" she said. "Go on till I tell you to stop."

So Elizabeth Ann, very much surprised but very much interested, read on, sentence after sentence, till she forgot they were sentences and just thought of what they meant. She read a whole page and then another page, and that was the end of the selection. She had never read aloud so much in her life. She was aware that everybody in the room had stopped working to listen to her. She felt proud and less afraid than she had ever thought she could be in a school-room. When she finished, "You read very well!" said the teacher. "Is this book easy for you?"

"Oh, *yes!*" said Elizabeth Ann.

"I guess, then, that you'd better not stay in this class," said the teacher. She took a book out of her desk. "See if you can read that."

Elizabeth Ann began in her usual school-reading style, very slow and monotonous, but this didn't seem like a "reader" at all. It was poetry, full of hard words that were fun to try to pronounce, and it was all about an old woman who would hang out an American flag, even though the town was full of rebel soldiers. She read faster and faster, getting more and more excited, till she broke out with "Halt!" in such a loud, spirited voice that the sound of it startled her. She stopped, fearing that she would be laughed at. But nobody laughed. They were all listening eagerly, even the little ones, with their eyes turned toward her.

"You might as well go on and let us see how it came out," said the teacher, and Betsy finished triumphantly.

"*Well*," said the teacher, "there's no sense in your reading along in the third reader. After this you'll recite out of the seventh reader with Frank and Harry and Stashie."

Elizabeth Ann could not believe her ears. To be "jumped" four grades in that casual way! It wasn't possible. She at once thought, however, of something that would prevent it entirely, and while Ellen was reading her page in a slow, careful little voice, Elizabeth Ann was feeling miserably that she must explain to the teacher why she couldn't read with the seventh-grade children. Oh, how she wished she could! When they stood up to go back to their seats she hesitated, hung her head, and looked very unhappy. "Did you want to say something to me?" asked the teacher, pausing with a bit of chalk in her hand.

The little girl went up to her desk and said, what she knew it was her duty to confess: "I can't be allowed to read in the seventh reader. I don't write a bit well, and I never get the mental number-work right. I couldn't do *anything* with seventh-grade arithmetic!"

The teacher looked blank and said: "*I* didn't say anything about your number-work! I don't *know* anything about it! You haven't recited yet." She turned away and began to write a list of words on the board. "Betsy, Ralph, and Ellen study their spelling," she said. "You little ones come up for your reading."

Two little boys and two little girls came forward as Elizabeth Ann began to con over the words on the board. At first she found she was listening to the little, chirping voices, as the children struggled with their reading, instead of studying "doubt," "travel," "cheese," and the other words in her lesson. But she put her hands over her ears, and her mind on her spelling. She wanted to make a good impression with that lesson. After a while, when she was sure she could spell them all correctly, she began to listen and look around her. She always "got" her spelling in less time than was allowed the class, and usually sat idle, looking out of the window until that study period was over. But now the moment she stopped staring at the board and moving her lips as she spelled to herself the teacher said, just as though she had been watching her every minute instead of conducting a class, "Betsy, have you learned your spelling?"

"Yes, ma'am, I think so," said Elizabeth Ann, wondering why she was asked.

"That's fine," said the teacher. "I wish you'd take little Molly over in that corner and help her with her reading. She's getting on so much better than the rest of the class that I hate to have her lose her time. Just hear her read the rest of her little story, will you, and don't help her unless she's really stuck."

Elizabeth Ann was startled by this request. She had

never heard of such a thing in a schoolroom. She felt very uncertain of herself as she sat down on a low chair in the corner away from the desks, with the child leaning on her knee. And yet she was not exactly afraid, either, because Molly was such a shy, tiny, roly-poly thing, with her crop of yellow curls, and her bright blue eyes so serious as she looked hard at the book and began: "Once there was a rat. It was a fat rat." No, it was impossible to be frightened of such a funny little girl, who peered so earnestly into the older child's face to make sure she was doing her lesson right.

Elizabeth Ann had never had anything to do with children younger than herself, and she felt very pleased and important to have anybody look up to *her!* She put her arm around Molly's square, warm, fat body and gave her a squeeze. Molly snuggled up closer, and the two children put their heads together over the printed page, Elizabeth Ann correcting Molly gently when she made a mistake, and waiting patiently when she hesitated. She had so fresh in her mind her own suffering from quick, nervous corrections that she took the greatest pleasure in speaking quietly and not interrupting the little girl more than was necessary. It was fun to teach, *lots* of fun! She was surprised when the teacher said, "Well, Betsy, how did Molly do?"

"Oh, is the time up?" said Elizabeth Ann. "Why, she does beautifully, I think, for such a little thing."

"Do you suppose," said the teacher thoughtfully, just as though Betsy were a grown-up person, "do you suppose she could go into the second reader, with Eliza? There's no use keeping her in the first if she's ready to go on."

Elizabeth Ann's head whirled with this second light-handed juggling with the sacred distinction between the grades. In the big brick schoolhouse nobody *ever* went into another grade except at the beginning of a new year, after you'd passed a lot of examinations. She had not known that anybody could do anything else. The idea that every-body took a year to a grade, no *matter* what! was so fixed in her mind that she felt as though the teacher had said: "How would you like to stop being nine years old and be twelve instead? And don't you think Molly would better be eight instead of six?"

However, just then her class in arithmetic was called, so that she had no more time to be puzzled. She came forward with Ralph and Ellen again, very low in her mind. She hated arithmetic with all her might, and she really didn't understand a thing about it! By long experience she had learned to read her teachers' faces very accurately, and she guessed by their expression whether the answer she gave was the right one. And that was the only way she could tell. You never heard of any other child who did that, did you?

They had mental arithmetic, of course (Elizabeth Ann thought it just her luck!), and of course it was those hateful eights and sevens, and of course right away poor Betsy got the one she hated most, 7×8. She never knew that one! She said dispiritedly that it was 54, remembering vaguely that it was somewhere in the fifties. Ralph burst out scorn-fully, "56!" and the teacher, as if she wanted to take him down for showing off, pounced on him with 9×8. He an-swered, without drawing breath, 72. Elizabeth Ann shuddered at his accuracy. Ellen, too, rose to the occasion when she got 6×7, which Elizabeth Ann could sometimes remember and sometimes not. And then, oh horrors! It was her turn again! Her turn had never before come more than twice during a mental arithmetic lesson. She was so startled by the swiftness with which the question went around that she balked on 6×6, which she knew perfectly. And before she could recover Ralph had answered and had rattled out a 108 in answer to 9×12; and then Ellen slapped down an 84 on top of 7×12. Good gracious! Who could have guessed, from the way they read, they could do their tables like this! She herself missed on 7×7 and was ready to cry. After this the teacher didn't call on her at all, but showered questions down on the other two, who sent the answers back with sickening speed.

After the lesson the teacher said, smiling, "Well, Betsy, you were right about your arithmetic. I guess you'd better recite with Eliza for a while. She's doing second-grade work. I shouldn't be surprised if, after a good review with her, you'd be able to go on with the third-grade work."

Elizabeth Ann fell back on the bench with her mouth open. She felt really dizzy. What crazy things the teacher said! She felt as though she was being pulled limb from limb.

"What's the matter?" asked the teacher, seeing her bewildered face.

"Why—why," said Elizabeth Ann, "I don't know what I am at all. If I'm second-grade arithmetic and seventh-grade reading and third-grade spelling, what grade *am* I?"

The teacher laughed. "*You* aren't any grade at all, no

matter where you are in school. You're just yourself, aren't you? What difference does it make what grade you're in? And what's the use of your reading little baby things too easy for you just because you don't know your multiplication table?"

"Well, for goodness' *sakes!*" ejaculated Elizabeth Ann, feeling very much as though somebody had stood her suddenly on her head.

"What's the matter?" asked the teacher again.

This time Elizabeth Ann didn't answer, because she herself didn't know what the matter was. But I do, and I'll tell you. The matter was that never before had she known what she was doing in school. She had always thought she was there to pass from one grade to another, and she was ever so startled to get a glimpse of the fact that she was there to learn how to read and write and cipher and generally use her mind, so she could take care of herself when she came to be grown up. Of course, she didn't know that 'til she did come to be grown up, but in that moment, she had her first dim notion of it, and it made her feel the way you do when you're learning to skate and somebody pulls away the chair you've been leaning on and says, "Now, go it alone!"

The teacher waited a minute. When Elizabeth Ann didn't say anything more, she rang a little bell. "Recess time," she said. As the children marched out and began putting on their wraps she followed them into the cloakroom, pulled on a warm, red cap and a red sweater, and ran outdoors herself. "Who's on my side!" she called, and the children came darting out after her. Elizabeth Ann had dreaded the first recess time with the strange children, but she had no time to feel shy, for in a twinkling she was on one end of a long rope with a lot of her schoolmates, pulling with all her might against the teacher and two of the big boys. Nobody had looked at her curiously, nobody had said anything to her beyond a loud, "Come on, Betsy!" from Ralph, who was at the head on their side.

They pulled and they pulled, digging their feet into the ground and bracing themselves against the rocks which stuck up out of the playground. Sometimes the teacher's side yanked them along by quick jerks, and then they'd all set their feet hard when Ralph shouted out, "Now, *all together!*" and they'd slowly drag the other side back. And all the time everybody was shouting and yelling together with the excitement. Betsy was screaming too, and when a wagon passing by stopped and a big, broad-shouldered farmer jumped down laughing, put the end of the rope over his shoulder, and walked off with the whole lot of them 'til he had pulled them clear off their feet, Elizabeth Ann found herself rolling over and over with a breathless, squirming mass of children, her laughter rising even above the shouts of the others. She laughed so she could hardly get up on her feet again, it was such an unexpected ending to the tug-of-war.

The big farmer was laughing too. "You ain't so smart as you *think* you are, are you!" he jeered at them good-naturedly. Then he started yelling "WHOA there!" to his horses, which had begun to walk on. He had to run after them with all his might, and just climbed into the back of the wagon and grabbed the reins the very moment they broke into a trot. The children laughed, and Ralph shouted after him, "Hi, there, Uncle Nate! Who's not so smart as he thinks he is, *now!*" He turned to the little girls near him. "They 'most got away from him *that* time!" he said. "He's awful foolish about leaving them standing while he's funning or something. He thinks he's awful funny, anyhow. Some day they'll run away on him and *then* where'll he be?"

Elizabeth Ann was thinking to herself that this was one of the queerest things that had happened to her even in this queer place. Never, why never once, had any grownup, passing the playground of the big brick building, *dreamed* of such a thing as stopping for a minute to play. They never even looked at the children, any more than if they were in another world. In fact she had felt the school was in another world.

"Ralph, it's your turn to get the water," said the teacher, handing him a pail. "Want to go along?" said Ralph gruffly to Ellen and Betsy. He led the way and the little girls walked after him. Now that she was out of a crowd Elizabeth Ann felt all her shyness come down on her like a black cloud, drying up her mouth and turning her hands and feet cold as ice. Into one of these cold hands she felt small, warm fingers slide. She looked down and there was little Molly trotting by her side, turning her blue eyes up trustfully. "Teacher says I can go with you if you'll take care of me," she said. "She never lets us first-graders go without somebody bigger to help us over the log."

As she spoke they came to a small, clear, swift brook, crossed by a big white-birch log. Elizabeth Ann was horri-

bly afraid to set foot on it, but with little Molly's hand
holding tightly to hers she was ashamed to say she was
afraid. Ralph skipped across, swinging the pail to show how
easy it was for him. Ellen followed more slowly, and then—
don't you wish Aunt Frances could have been there!—
Betsy shut her teeth together hard, put Molly ahead of her,
took her hand, and started across. As a matter of fact Molly
went along as sure-footed as a little goat, having done it a
hundred times, and it was she who steadied Elizabeth Ann.
But nobody knew this, Molly least of all.

Ralph took a drink out of a tin cup standing on a stump
near by, dipped the pail into a deep, clear pool, and started
back to the school. Ellen took a drink and offered the cup
to Betsy, very shyly, without looking up. After they had all
three had a drink they stood there for a moment, much
embarrassed. Then Ellen said, in a small voice, "Do you
like dolls with yellow hair the best?"

Now it happened that Elizabeth Ann had very positive
convictions on this point which she had never spoken of,
because Aunt Frances didn't *really* care about dolls. She
only pretended to, to be company for her little niece.

"No, I *don't!*" answered the little girl emphatically. "I
get just sick and tired of always seeing them with that old,
bright yellow hair! I like them to have brown hair, just the
way most little girls do!"

Ellen lifted her eyes and smiled radiantly. "Oh, so do I!"
she said. "And that lovely old doll your folks have has got
brown hair. Will you let me play with her some time?"

"My folks?" said Elizabeth Ann blankly.

"Why, yes, your Aunt Abigail and your Uncle Henry."

"Have they got a *doll?*" said Betsy, thinking this was the very climax of Putney queerness.

"Oh, my, yes!" said Molly eagerly. "She's the one Mrs. Putney had when she was a little girl. And she's got the loveliest clothes! She's in the hair trunk under the eaves in the attic. They let me take her down once when I was there with Mother. And Mother said she guessed, now a little girl had come there to live, they'd let you have her down all the time. I'll bring mine over next Saturday, if you want me to. Mine's got yellow hair, but she's real pretty anyhow. If Father's going to mill that day, he can leave me there for the morning."

Elizabeth Ann had not understood more than one word in five of this, but the school bell rang and they went back, little Molly helping Elizabeth Ann over the log and thinking she was being helped, as before.

They ran along to the little building, and there I'm going to leave them, because I think I've told enough about their school for *one* while. It was only a poor, rough, district school anyway, that no city Superintendent of Schools would have looked at for a minute, except to sniff.

If You Don't
Like Conversation
in a Book
Skip This Chapter!

Betsy opened the door and was greeted by her kitten, who ran to her, purring and arching her back to be stroked.

"Well," said Aunt Abigail, looking up from the pan of apples in her lap, "I suppose you're starved, aren't you! Get yourself a piece of bread and butter, why don't you, and have one of these apples."

As the little girl sat down by her, munching fast on this provender, she asked: "What desk did you get?"

Elizabeth Ann thought for a moment, cuddling Eleanor up to her face. "I think it is the third from the front in the second row." She wondered why Aunt Abigail cared.

"Oh, I guess that's your Uncle Henry's desk. It's the one

his father had, too. Are there a couple of H.P.'s carved on it?"

Betsy nodded.

"His father carved the H.P. on the lid, so Henry had to put his inside. I remember the winter he put it there. It was the first season Mother let me wear real hoop skirts. I sat in the first seat on the third row."

Betsy ate her apple more and more slowly, trying to take in what Aunt Abigail had said. Uncle Henry and *his father* —why Moses or Alexander the Great didn't seem any further back in the mists of time to Elizabeth Ann than did Uncle Henry's *father!* And to think he had been a little boy, right there at that desk! She stopped chewing altogether for a moment and stared into space. Although she was only nine years old, she was feeling a little of the same rapt wonder that people in the past were really people, which makes a first visit to the Roman Forum a thrilling event for grownups. That very desk!

After a moment she came to herself, and finding some apple still in her mouth, went on chewing meditatively. "Aunt Abigail," she said, "how long ago was that?"

"Let's see," said the old woman, peeling apples with wonderful rapidity. "I was born in 1844. And I was six when I first went to school. That's sixty-six years ago."

Elizabeth Ann, like all little girls of nine, had very little notion how long sixty-six years might be. "Was George Washington alive then?" she asked.

The wrinkles around Aunt Abigail's eyes deepened mirthfully, but she did not laugh as she answered, "No, that was long after he died, but the schoolhouse was there when he was alive."

"It *was!*" said Betsy, staring, her teeth set deep in her apple.

"Yes, indeed. It was the first house in the valley built of sawed lumber. You know, when our folks came up here, they had to build all their houses of logs to begin with."

"They *did!*" cried Betsy, with her mouth full of apple.

"Why, yes, child, what else did you suppose they had to make houses out of? They had to have something to live in, right off. The sawmills came later."

"I didn't know anything about it," said Betsy. "Tell me about it."

"Why, you knew, didn't you—your Aunt Harriet must have told you—about how our folks came up here from Connecticut in 1763, on horseback? Connecticut was an old settled place then, compared to Vermont. There wasn't anything here but trees and bears and wood pigeons. I've heard 'em say that the wood pigeons were so thick you could go out after dark and club 'em out of the trees, just like hens roosting in a henhouse. There always was cold pigeon pie in the pantry, just the way we have doughnuts. And they used bear grease to grease their boots and their hair, bears were so plenty. It sounds like good eating, doesn't it! But of course that was just at first. It got quite settled up before long, and by the time of the Revolution, bears were getting pretty scarce, and soon the wood pigeons were all gone."

"And the schoolhouse—that schoolhouse where I went

today—was that built *then?*" Elizabeth Ann found it hard
to believe.

"Yes, it used to have a great big chimney and fireplace in
it. It was built long before stoves were invented, you
know."

"Why, I thought stoves were *always* invented!" cried
Elizabeth Ann. This was the most startling and interesting
conversation she had ever taken part in.

Aunt Abigail laughed. "Mercy, no, child! Why, *I* can
remember when only folks that were pretty well off had
stoves and real poor people still cooked over a hearth fire. I
always thought it a pity they tore down the big chimney
and fireplace out of the schoolhouse and put in that big,
ugly stove. But folks are so daft over newfangled things.
Well, anyhow, they couldn't take away the sundial on the
window sill. You want to be sure to look at that. It's on the
sill of the middle window on the right hand as you face the
teacher's desk."

"Sundial," repeated Betsy. "What's that?"

"Why, to tell the time by, when—"

"Why didn't they have a clock?" asked the child.

Aunt Abigail laughed. "Good gracious, there was only
one clock in the valley for years and years, and that belonged to the Wardons, the rich family in the village. Most
people had sundials cut in their window sills. There's one
on the window sill of our pantry this minute. Come on, I'll
show it to you." She got up heavily with her pan of apples,
and trotted briskly, shaking the floor as she went, over to
the stove. "But first just watch me put these on to cook so
you'll know how." She set the pan on the stove, poured

some water from the teakettle over the apples, and put on a cover. "Now come on into the pantry."

They entered a sweet-smelling, spicy small room, all white paint and shelves which were loaded with dishes and boxes and bags and pans of milk and jars of preserves.

"There!" said Aunt Abigail, opening the window. "That's not so good as the one at school. This only tells when noon is."

Elizabeth Ann stared stupidly at the deep scratch on the window sill.

"Don't you see?" said Aunt Abigail. "When the shadow got to that mark it was noon. And the rest of the time you guessed by how far it was from the mark. Let's see if I can come anywhere near it now." She looked at it hard and said: "I guess it's half-past four." She glanced back into the kitchen at the clock and said: "Oh, pshaw! It's ten minutes past five! Now my grandmother could have told that within five minutes, just by the place of the shadow. I declare! Sometimes it seems to me that every time a new piece of machinery comes into the door some of our wits fly out at the window! Now I couldn't any more live without matches than I could fly! And yet they all used to get along all right before they had matches. Makes me feel foolish to think I'm not smart enough to get along, if I *wanted* to, without those little snips of pine and brimstone. Here, Betsy, take a cookie. It's against my principles to let a child leave the pantry without having a cookie. My! it does seem like living again to have a young one around to stuff!"

Betsy took the cookie, but went on with the conversation by exclaiming, "*How* could *any*body get along without matches? You *have* to have matches."

Aunt Abigail didn't answer at first. They were back in the kitchen now. She was looking at the clock again. "See here," she said; "it's time I began getting supper ready. We divide up on the work. Ann gets the dinner and I get the supper. And everybody gets his own breakfast. Which would you rather do, help Ann with the dinner, or me with the supper?"

Elizabeth Ann had not had the slightest idea of helping anybody with any meal, but, confronted unexpectedly with the alternative offered, she made up her mind so quickly that she didn't want to help Cousin Ann, and declared so loudly, "Oh, help *you* with the supper!" that her promptness made her sound quite hearty and willing. "Well, that's fine," said Aunt Abigail. "We'll set the table now. But first you would better look at that applesauce. I hear it walloping away as though it was boiling too fast. Maybe you'd better push it back where it won't cook so fast. There are the holders, on that hook."

Elizabeth Ann approached the stove with the holder in her hand and horror in her heart. Nobody had ever dreamed of asking her to handle hot things. She looked around dismally at Aunt Abigail, but the old woman was standing with her back turned, doing something at the kitchen table. Very gingerly the little girl took hold of the handle of the saucepan, and very gingerly she shoved it to the back of the stove. And then she stood still a moment to admire herself. She could do that as well as anybody!

"Why," said Aunt Abigail, as if remembering that Betsy

had asked her a question, "any man could strike a spark from his flint and steel that he had for his gun. And he'd keep striking it till it happened to fly out in the right direction, and you'd catch it in some fluff where it would start a smolder, and you'd blow on it till you got a little flame, and drop tiny bits of shaved-up dry pine in it, and so, little by little, you'd build your fire up."

"But it must have taken for*ever* to do that!"

"Oh, you didn't have to do that more than once in ever so long," said Aunt Abigail, briskly. She interrupted her story to say: "Now you put the silver around, while I cream the potatoes. It's in that drawer—a knife, a fork, and two spoons for each place—and the plates and cups are up there behind the glass doors. We're going to have hot cocoa again tonight." As the little girl, hypnotized by the other's casual, offhand way of issuing instruction, began to fumble with the knives and forks she went on: "Why, you'd start your fire that way, and then you'd never let it go out. Everybody that amounted to anything knew how to bank the hearth fire with ashes at night so it would be sure to last. And the first thing in the morning, you got down on your knees and poked the ashes away very carefully till you got to the hot coals. Then you'd blow with the bellows and drop in pieces of dry pine—don't forget the water glasses— and you'd blow gently till they flared up and the shavings caught, and there your fire would be kindled again. The napkins are in the second drawer."

Betsy went on setting the table, deep in thought, reconstructing the old life. As she put the napkins around she said, "But *sometimes* it must have gone out . . ."

"Yes," said Aunt Abigail, "sometimes it went out, and then one of the children was sent over to the nearest neighbor to borrow some fire. He'd take a covered iron pan fastened on to a long hickory stick, and go through the woods—everything was woods then—to the next house and wait till they had their fire going and could spare him a pan full of coals; and then—don't forget the salt and pepper—he would leg it home as fast as he could streak it, to get there before the coals went out. Say, Betsy, I think that applesauce is ready to be sweetened. You do it, will you? I've got my hands in the biscuit dough. The sugar's in the left-hand drawer in the kitchen cabinet."

"Oh, *my!*" cried Betsy, dismayed. "*I* don't know how to cook!"

Aunt Abigail laughed and put back a strand of curly white hair with the back of her floury hand. "You know how to stir sugar into your cup of cocoa, don't you?"

"But how *much* shall I put in?" asked Elizabeth Ann, clamoring for exact instruction so she wouldn't need to do any thinking for herself.

"Till it tastes right," said Aunt Abigail, carelessly. "Fix it to suit yourself, and I guess the rest of us will like it. Take that big spoon to stir it with."

Elizabeth Ann took off the lid and began stirring in sugar, a teaspoonful at a time, but she soon saw that that made no impression. She poured in a cupful, stirred it vigorously, and tasted it. Better, but not quite enough. She put in a tablespoonful more and tasted it, staring off into space as she concentrated her attention on the taste. It was quite a responsibility to prepare the applesauce for a family.

It was ever so good, too. But maybe a *little* more sugar. She put in a teaspoonful and decided it was just exactly right!

"Done?" asked Aunt Abigail. "Take it off, then, and pour it out in that big yellow bowl, and put it on the table in front of your place. You've made it; you ought to serve it."

"It isn't done, is it?" asked Betsy. "That isn't *all* you do to make applesauce!"

"What else could you do?" asked Aunt Abigail.

"Well . . . !" said Elizabeth Ann, very much surprised. "I didn't know it was so easy to cook!"

"Easiest thing in the world," said Aunt Abigail gravely, with the merry wrinkles around her merry old eyes all creased up with silent fun.

When Uncle Henry came in from the barn, with old Shep at his heels, and Cousin Ann came down from upstairs, where her sewing machine had been humming like a big bee, they were both duly impressed when told that Betsy had set the table and made the applesauce. They pronounced it very good applesauce indeed, and each sent his saucer back to the little girl for a second helping. She herself ate three saucerfuls. Her own private opinion was that it was the very best applesauce ever made.

After supper was over and the dishes washed and wiped, Betsy helping with the putting-away, the four gathered around the big lamp on the table with the red cover. Cousin Ann was making some buttonholes in the shirt-waist she had constructed that afternoon, Aunt Abigail was darning socks, and Uncle Henry was mending a piece

of harness. Shep lay on the couch and snored until he got
so noisy they couldn't stand it, and Cousin Ann poked him
in the ribs and he woke up snorting and gurgling and looking around sheepishly. Every time this happened it made
Betsy laugh. She held Eleanor, who didn't snore at all, but
made the prettiest tea-kettle-singing purr deep in her
throat, and opened and sheathed her needle-like claws in
Betsy's dress.

"Well, how'd you get on at school?" asked Uncle Henry.

"I've got your desk," said Elizabeth Ann, looking at him
curiously, at his gray hair and wrinkled, weather-beaten
face, and trying to think what he must have looked like
when he was a little boy like Ralph.

"So?" said Uncle Henry. "Well, let me tell you that's a
mighty good desk! Did you notice the deep groove in the
top of it?"

Betsy nodded. She had wondered what that was used for.

"Well, that was the lead pencil desk in the old days.
When they couldn't run down to the store to buy things,
because there wasn't any store to run to, how do you suppose they got their lead pencils?"

Elizabeth Ann shook her head, incapable even of a
guess. She had never thought before but that lead pencils
grew in glass showcases in stores.

"Well, sir," said Uncle Henry, "I'll tell you. They took a
piece off the lump of lead they made their bullets of,
melted it over the fire in the hearth down at the schoolhouse till it would run like water, and poured it in that
groove. When it cooled off, there was a long streak of solid
lead, about as big as one of our lead pencils nowadays.

They'd break that up in shorter lengths, and there you'd have your lead pencils, made while you wait. I tell you, in the old days folks knew how to take care of themselves more than now."

"Why, weren't there any stores?" asked Elizabeth Ann. She could not imagine living without buying things at stores.

"Where'd they get the things to put in a store in those days?" asked Uncle Henry, argumentatively. "Every single thing had to be lugged clear from Albany or from Connecticut on horseback."

"Why didn't they use wagons?" asked Elizabeth Ann.

"You can't run a wagon unless you've got a road to run it on, can you?" asked Uncle Henry. "It was a long, long time before they had any roads. It's an awful chore to make roads in a new country all woods and hills and swamps and rocks. You were lucky if there was a good path from your house to the next settlement."

"Now, Henry," said Aunt Abigail, "do stop going on about old times long enough to let Betsy answer the question you asked her. You haven't given her a chance to say how she got on at school."

"Well, I'm *awfully* mixed up!" said Betsy, complainingly. "I don't know what I am! I'm second-grade arithmetic and third-grade spelling and seventh-grade reading and I don't know what in writing or composition. We didn't have those."

Nobody seemed to think this very remarkable, or even very interesting. Uncle Henry, indeed, noted it only to say, "Seventh-grade reading!" He turned to Aunt Abigail.

"Oh, Mother, don't you suppose she could read aloud to us evenings?"

Aunt Abigail and Cousin Ann both laid down their sewing to laugh! "Yes, yes, Father, and play checkers with you too, like as not!" They explained to Betsy: "Your Uncle Henry is just daft on being read aloud to when he's got something to do in the evening, and when he hasn't, he's as fidgety as a broody hen if he can't play checkers. Ann hates checkers and I haven't got the time, often."

"Oh, I *love* to play checkers!" said Betsy.

"Well, *now* . . ." said Uncle Henry, rising instantly and dropping his half-mended harness on the table. "Let's have a game."

"Oh, Father!" said Cousin Ann, in the tone she used for Shep. "How about that piece of breeching! You know that's not safe. Why don't you finish that up first?"

Uncle Henry sat down again, looking as Shep did when Cousin Ann told him to lie down on the couch, and took up his needle and awl.

"But I could read something aloud," said Betsy, feeling very sorry for him. "At least I think I could. I never did, except at school."

"What shall we have, Mother?" asked Uncle Henry eagerly.

"Oh, I don't know. What have we got in this bookcase?" said Aunt Abigail. "It's pretty cold to go into the parlor to the other one." She leaned forward, ran her fat forefinger over the worn old volumes, and took out a battered, blue-covered book. "Scott?"

"Gosh, yes!" said Uncle Henry, his eyes shining. "The staggit eve!"

At least that was the way it sounded to Betsy, but when she took the book and looked where Aunt Abigail pointed she read it correctly, though in a timid, uncertain voice. She was proud to think she could please a grown-up so much as she was evidently pleasing Uncle Henry, but the idea of reading aloud for people to hear, not for a teacher to correct, was unheard-of.

> *The Stag at eve had drunk his fill*
> *Where danced the moon on Monan's rill,*

she began, and it was as though she had stepped into a boat and was swept off by a strong current. She did not know what all the words meant, and she could not pronounce a good many of the names, but nobody interrupted to correct her, and she read on and on, steadied by the strongly marked rhythm, drawn forward swiftly from one clanging, sonorous rhyme to another. Uncle Henry nodded his head in time to the rise and fall of her voice and now and then stopped his work to look at her with bright, eager, old eyes. He knew some of the places by heart evidently, for once in a while his voice would join the little girl's for a couplet or two. They chanted together thus:

> *A moment listened to the cry*
> *That thickened as the chase drew nigh,*
> *Then, as the headmost foes appeared,*
> *With one brave bound, the copse he cleared.*

At the last line Uncle Henry flung his arm out wide, and the child felt as though the deer had made his great leap there, before her eyes.

"I've seen 'em jump just like that," broke in Uncle Henry. "A two-three-hundred-pound stag go up over a four-foot fence just like a piece of thistledown in the wind."

"Uncle Henry," asked Elizabeth Ann, "what is a copse?"

"I don't know," said Uncle Henry indifferently. "Something in the woods, must be. Underbrush most likely. You can always tell words you don't know by the sense of the whole thing. Go on."

> *And stretching forward, free and far,*

The child's voice took up the chant again. She read faster and faster as it got more exciting. Uncle Henry joined in on:

> *For, jaded now and spent with toil,*
> *Embossed with foam and dark with soil,*
> *While every gasp with sobs he drew,*
> *The laboring stag strained full in view.*

The little girl's heart beat fast. She fled along through the next lines, stumbling desperately over the hard words but seeing the headlong chase through them clearly as through tree trunks in a forest. Uncle Henry broke in in a triumphant shout:

The wily quarry shunned the shock
And turned him from the opposing rock;
Then dashing down a darksome glen,
Soon lost to hound the hunter's ken,
In the deep Trossach's wildest nook
His solitary refuge took.

"Oh, *my!*" cried Elizabeth Ann, laying down the book. "He got away, didn't he? I was *so* afraid he wouldn't!"

"I can just hear those dogs yelping, can't you?" said Uncle Henry.

Yelled on the view the opening pack.

"Sometimes you hear 'em that way up on the slope of Hemlock Mountain back of us, when they get to running a deer."

"What say we have some popcorn?" suggested Aunt Abigail. "Betsy, don't you want to pop us some?"

"I never *did,*" said the little girl, but in a less doubtful tone than she had ever used with that phrase so familiar to her. A dim notion was growing in her mind that the fact that she had never done a thing was no proof that she couldn't.

"I'll show you," said Uncle Henry. He reached down a couple of ears of corn from a big yellow cluster hanging on the wall, and he and Betsy shelled them into the popper, popped it full of snowy kernels, buttered it, salted it, and took it back to the table.

It was just as she was eating her first ambrosial mouthful

that the door opened and a fur-capped head was thrust in.
A man's voice said: "Evenin', folks. No, I can't stay. I was
down at the village just now, and thought I'd ask for any
mail down our way." He tossed a newspaper and a letter on
the table and was gone.

The letter was addressed to Elizabeth Ann and it was
from Aunt Frances. She read it to herself while Uncle
Henry read the newspaper. Aunt Frances wrote that she
had been perfectly horrified to learn that Cousin Molly had
not kept Elizabeth Ann with her, and that she would never
forgive her for that cruelty. And when she thought that
her darling was at Putney Farm! . . . Her blood ran cold.
It positively did! It was too dreadful. But it couldn't be
helped, for a time anyhow, because Aunt Harriet was really
very sick. Elizabeth Ann would have to be a dear, brave
child and endure it as best she could. And as soon . . .
oh, as soon as ever she *could*, Aunt Frances would come
and take her away from them. "Don't cry *too* much, darling
. . . it breaks my heart to think of you there! *Try* to be
cheerful, dearest! *Try* to bear it for the sake of your distracted, loving Aunt Frances."

Elizabeth Ann looked up from this letter and across the
table at Aunt Abigail's rosy, wrinkled old face, bent over
her darning. Uncle Henry laid the paper down, took a big
mouthful of popcorn, and beat time silently with his hand.
When he could speak he murmured:

> An hundred dogs bayed deep and strong,
> Clattered an hundred steeds along.

Old Shep woke up with a snort and Aunt Abigail fed him a handful of popcorn. Little Eleanor stirred in her sleep, stretched, yawned, and nestled down into a ball again on the little girl's lap. Betsy could feel in her own body the rhythmic vibration of the kitten's contented purr.

Aunt Abigail looked up: "Finished your letter? I hope Harriet is no worse. What does Frances say?"

Elizabeth Ann blushed a deep red and crushed the letter together in her hand. She felt ashamed and she did not know why. "Aunt Frances says . . . Aunt Frances says . . ." she began, hesitating. "She says Aunt Harriet is still pretty sick." She stopped, drew a long breath, and went on, "And she sends her love to you."

Now Aunt Frances hadn't done anything of the kind, so this was a really whopping fib. But Elizabeth Ann didn't care if it was. It made her feel less ashamed, though she didn't know why. She took another mouthful of popcorn and stroked Eleanor's back.

Uncle Henry got up and stretched. "It's time to go to bed, folks," he said. As he wound the clock Betsy heard him murmuring:

But when the sun his beacon red . . .

Elizabeth Ann
Fails in an
Examination

I wonder if you can guess the name of a little girl who, about a month after this, was walking along through the melting snow in the woods with a big black dog running circles around her. Yes, all alone in the woods with a terrible great dog beside her, and yet not a bit afraid. You don't suppose it could be Elizabeth Ann? Well, who-ever she was, she had something on her mind, for she walked more and more slowly and had only a very absent-minded pat for the dog's head when he thrust it up for a caress. When the wood road led into a clearing in which there was a rough little house of slabs, the child stopped altogether, and, looking down, began nervously to draw lines in the snow with her overshoe.

You see, something perfectly dreadful had happened in school that day. The Superintendent, the all-important, seldom-seen Superintendent, came to visit the school and the children were given some examination so he could see how they were getting on.

Now, you know what an examination did to Elizabeth Ann. Or haven't I told you yet?

Well, if I haven't, it's because words fail me. If there is anything horrid that an examination *didn't* do to Elizabeth Ann, I have yet to hear of it. It began years ago, before ever she went to school, when she heard Aunt Frances talking about how *she* had dreaded examinations when she was a child, and how they dried up her mouth and made her ears ring and her head ache and her knees get all weak and her mind a perfect blank, so that she didn't know what two and two made. Of course Elizabeth Ann didn't feel *all* those things right off at her first examination, but by the time she had had several and had rushed to tell Aunt Frances about how awful they were and the two of them had sympathized with one another and compared symptoms and then wept about her resulting low marks, why, she not only had all the symptoms Aunt Frances had ever had, but a good many more of her own invention.

Well, she had had them all and had them hard this afternoon, when the Superintendent was there. Her mouth had gone dry and her knees had shaken and her elbows had felt as though they had no more bones in them than so much jelly, and her eyes had smarted, and oh, what answers she had made! That dreadful tight panic had clutched at her throat whenever the Superintendent had looked at her, and she had disgraced herself ten times over. She went hot and cold to think of it, and felt quite sick with hurt vanity. She who did so well every day and was so much looked-up-to by her classmates, what *must* they be thinking of her! To tell the truth, she had been crying as she walked along through the woods, because she was so sorry for herself. Her eyes were all red still, and her throat sore from the big lump in it.

And now she would live it all over again as she told the Putney cousins. For of course they must be told. She had always told Aunt Frances everything that happened in school. It happened that Aunt Abigail had been taking a nap when she got home from school, and so she had come out to the sap house, where Cousin Ann and Uncle Henry were making syrup, to have it over with as soon as possible. She went up to the little slab house now, dragging her feet and hanging her head, and opened the door.

Cousin Ann, in a very short old skirt and a man's coat and high rubber boots, was just poking some more wood into the big fire which blazed furiously under the broad, flat pan where the sap was boiling. The rough, brown hut was filled with white steam and that sweetest of all odors, hot maple syrup. Cousin Ann turned her head, her face red with the heat of the fire, and nodded at the child.

"Hello, Betsy, you're just in time. I've saved out a cupful of hot syrup for you, all ready to wax."

Betsy hardly heard this, although she had been wild about waxed sugar on snow ever since her very first taste of it. "Cousin Ann," she said unhappily, "the Superintendent visited our school this afternoon."

"Did he?" said Cousin Ann, dipping a thermometer into the boiling syrup.

"Yes, and we had *examinations!*" said Betsy.

"Did you?" said Cousin Ann, holding the thermometer up to the light and looking at it.

"And you know how perfectly awful examinations make you feel," said Betsy, very near to tears again.

"Why, no," said Cousin Ann, sorting over syrup tins. "They never made me feel awful. I thought they were sort of fun."

"*Fun!*" cried Betsy, indignantly, staring through the beginnings of her tears.

"Why, yes. Like taking a dare, don't you know. Somebody stumps you to jump off the hitching post, and you do it to show 'em. I always used to think examinations were like that. Somebody stumps you to spell 'pneumonia,' and you do it to show 'em. Here's your cup of syrup. You'd better go right out and wax it while it's hot."

Elizabeth Ann automatically took the cup in her hand, but she did not look at it. "But supposing you get so scared you can't spell 'pneumonia' or anything else!" she said feelingly. "That's what happened to me. You know how your mouth gets all dry and your knees . . ." She stopped. Cousin Ann had said she did *not* know all about those things. "Well, anyhow, I got so scared I could hardly stand *up!* And I made the most awful mistakes—things I know just as *well!* I spelled 'doubt' without any b and 'separate' with an e, and I said Iowa was bounded on the north by *Wisconsin*, and I . . ."

"Oh, well," said Cousin Ann, "it doesn't matter if you really know the right answers, does it? That's the important thing."

This was an idea which had never in all her life entered

Betsy's brain and she did not take it in now. She only shook her head miserably and went on in a doleful tone. "And I said 13 and 8 are 22! and I wrote March without any capital M, and I . . ."

"Look here, Betsy, do you *want* to tell me all this?" Cousin Ann spoke in the quick, ringing voice she had once in a while which made everybody, from old Shep up, open his eyes and get his wits about him. Betsy gathered hers and thought hard; and she came to an unexpected conclusion. No, she didn't really want to tell Cousin Ann all about it. Why was she doing it? Because she thought that was the thing to do. "Because if you don't really want to," went on Cousin Ann, "I don't see that it's doing anybody any good. I guess Hemlock Mountain will stand right there just the same even if you did forget to put a b in 'doubt.' And your syrup will be too cool to wax right if you don't take it out pretty soon."

She turned back to stroke the fire, and Elizabeth Ann, in a daze, found herself walking out of the door. It fell shut after her, and there she was under the clear, pale-blue sky, with the sun just hovering over the rim of Hemlock Mountain. She looked up at the big mountains, all blue and silver with shadows and snow, and wondered what in the world Cousin Ann had meant. Of course Hemlock Mountain would stand there just the same. But what of it? What did that have to do with her arithmetic, with anything? She had failed in her examination, hadn't she?

She found a clean white snowbank under a pine tree, and, setting her cup of syrup down in a safe place, began to pat the snow down hard to make the right bed for the waxing of the syrup. The sun, very hot for that late March day, brought out strongly the tarry perfume of the big pine tree. Near her the sap dripped musically into a bucket, already half full, hung on a maple tree. A blue jay rushed suddenly through the upper branches of the wood, his screaming and chattering voice sounding like noisy children at play.

Elizabeth Ann took up her cup and poured some of the thick, hot syrup out on the hard snow, making loops and curves as she poured. It stiffened and hardened at once, and she lifted up a great coil of it, threw her head back, and let it drop into her mouth. Concentrated sweetness of summer days was in that mouthful, part of it still hot and aromatic, part of it icy and wet with melting snow. She crunched it all together into a delicious big lump and sucked on it dreamily, her eyes on the rim of Hemlock Mountain, high above her there, the snow on it bright golden in the sunlight. Uncle Henry had promised to take her up to the top as soon as the snow went off. She wondered what the top of a mountain would be like. Uncle Henry had said the main thing was that you could see so much of the world at once. He said it was too queer the way your own house and big barn and great fields looked like little toy things that weren't of any account. It was because you could see so much more than just the . . .

She heard an imploring whine, and a cold nose was thrust into her hand! Why, there was old Shep begging for his share of waxed sugar. He loved it, though it did stick to his teeth so! She poured out another lot and gave half of it to Shep. It immediately stuck his jaws together tight, and he began pawing at his mouth and shaking his head till Betsy had to laugh. Then he managed to pull his jaws apart and chewed loudly and visibly, tossing his head, opening his mouth wide till Betsy could see the sticky, brown candy draped in melting festoons all over his big white teeth and red gullet. Then with a gulp he had swallowed it all down and was whining for more, striking softly at the little girl's skirt with his forepaw. "Oh, you eat it too fast!" cried Betsy, but she shared her next lot with him too. The sun had gone down over Hemlock Mountain by this time, and the big slope above her was all deep blue shadow. The mountain looked much higher now as the dusk began to fall, and loomed up bigger and bigger as though it reached to the sky. It was no wonder houses looked small from its top. Betsy ate the last of her sugar, looking up at the quiet giant there, towering grandly above her. There was no lump in her throat now. Although she still thought she did not know what in the world Cousin Ann meant by saying that about Hemlock Mountain and her examination, it's my opinion that she had made a good beginning of an understanding.

She was just picking up her cup to take it back to the sap house when Shep growled a little and stood with his ears and tail up, looking down the road. Something was coming down that road in the blue, clear twilight, something that was making a very queer noise. It sounded almost like somebody crying. It *was* somebody crying! It was a child crying. It was a little, little girl. . . . Betsy could see her now . . . stumbling along and crying as though her heart would break. Why, it was little Molly, her own particular charge at school, whose reading lesson she heard every day. Betsy and Shep ran to meet her. "What's the matter, Molly? What's the matter?" Betsy knelt down and put her arms around the weeping child. "Did you fall down? Did you hurt yourself? What are you doing way off here? Did you lose your way?"

"I don't want to go away! I don't want to go away!" said Molly over and over, clinging tightly to Betsy. It was a long time before Betsy could quiet her enough to find out what had happened. Then she made out between Molly's sobs that her mother had been taken suddenly sick and had to go away to a hospital, and that left nobody at home to take care of Molly, and she was to be sent away to some strange relatives in the city who didn't want her at all and who said so right out. . . .

Elizabeth Ann knew all about that! Her heart swelled big with sympathy. For a moment she stood again out on the sidewalk in front of the Lathrop house with old Mrs. Lathrop's ungracious white head bobbing from a window, and knew again that ghastly feeling of being unwanted. She knew why little Molly was crying! And she shut her hands together hard and made up her mind that she *would* help her out!

Do you know what she did, right off, without thinking about it? She didn't go and look up Aunt Abigail. She didn't wait till Uncle Henry came back from his round of emptying sap buckets into the big tub on his sled. As fast as her feet could carry her she flew back to Cousin Ann in the sap house. I can't tell you (except again that Cousin Ann was Cousin Ann) why it was that Betsy ran so fast to her and was so sure that everything would be all right as soon as Cousin Ann knew about it; but whatever the reason was it was a good one, for, though Cousin Ann did not stop to kiss Molly or even to look at her more than one sharp first glance, she said after a moment's pause, during which she filled a syrup can and screwed the cover down very tight: "Well, if her folks will let her stay, how would you like to have Molly come and stay with us till her mother gets back from the hospital? Now you've got a room of your own, I guess if you wanted to you could have her sleep with you."

"Oh, Molly, Molly, *Molly!*" shouted Betsy, jumping up and down, and then hugging the little girl with all her might. "Oh, it will be like having a little sister!"

Cousin Ann sounded a dry, warning note: "Don't be too sure her folks will let her. We don't know about them yet."

Betsy ran to her, and caught her hand, looking up at her with shining eyes. "Cousin Ann, if *you* go to see them and ask them, they will!"

This made even Cousin Ann give a little abashed smile of pleasure, although she made her face grave again at once and said: "You'd better go along back to the house now, Betsy. It's time for you to help Mother with the supper."

The two children trotted back along the darkening wood road, Shep running before them, little Molly clinging fast to the older child's hand. "Aren't you ever afraid, Betsy, in the woods this way?" she asked admiringly, looking about her with timid eyes.

"Oh, no!" said Betsy, protectingly, "there's nothing to be afraid of, except getting off on the wrong fork of the road, near the Wolf Pit."

"Oh, *ow!*" said Molly, scringing. "What's the Wolf Pit? What an awful name!"

Betsy laughed. She tried to make her laugh sound brave like Cousin Ann's, which always seemed so scornful of being afraid. As a matter of fact, she was beginning to fear that they *had* made the wrong turn, and she was not quite sure that she could find the way home. But she put this out of her mind and walked along very fast, peering ahead into the dusk. "It hasn't anything to do with wolves," she said in answer to Molly's question, "anyhow, not now. It's just a big, deep hole in the ground where a brook had dug out a cave. . . . Uncle Henry told me all about it when he showed it to me . . . and then part of the roof caved in; sometimes there's ice in the corner of the covered part all the summer, Aunt Abigail says."

"Why do you call it the Wolf Pit?" asked Molly, walking very close to Betsy and holding very tightly to her hand.

"Oh, long, ever so long ago, when the first settlers came up here, they heard a wolf howling all night, and when it didn't stop in the morning, they came up here on the mountain and found a wolf had fallen in and couldn't get out."

"My! I hope they killed him!" said Molly.

"Gracious! That was more than a hundred years ago," said Betsy. She was not thinking of what she was saying. She was thinking that if they *were* on the right road they ought to be home by this time. She was thinking that the right road ran downhill to the house all the way, and that this certainly seemed to be going up a little. She was wondering what had become of Shep. "Stand here just a minute, Molly," she said. "I want . . . I just want to go ahead a little bit and see . . . and see . . ." She darted on around a curve of the road and stood still, her heart sinking. The road turned there and led straight up the mountain!

For just a moment the little girl felt a wild impulse to burst out in a shriek for Aunt Frances, and to run crazily away, anywhere so long as she was running. But the thought of Molly standing back there, trustfully waiting to be taken care of, shut Betsy's lips together hard before her scream of fright got out. She stood still, thinking. Now she mustn't get frightened. All they had to do was to walk back along the road till they came to the fork and then make the right turn. But what if they didn't get back to the turn till it was so dark they couldn't see it? . . . Well, she mustn't think of that. She ran back, calling, "Come on, Molly," in a tone she tried to make as firm as Cousin Ann's. "I guess we have made the wrong turn after all. We'd better . . ."

But there was no Molly there. In the brief moment Betsy had stood thinking, Molly had disappeared. The long, shadowy wood road held not a trace of her.

Then Betsy *was* frightened and then she *did* begin to scream, at the top of her voice, "Molly! Molly!" She was beside herself with terror, and started back hastily to hear Molly's voice, very faint, apparently coming from the ground under her feet.

"Ow! Ow! Betsy! Get me out! Get me out!"

"Where *are* you?" shrieked Betsy.

"I don't know!" came Molly's sobbing voice. "I just

moved the least little bit out of the road, and slipped on the ice and began to slide and I couldn't stop myself and I fell down into a deep hole!"

Betsy's head felt as though her hair was standing up straight on end with horror. Molly must have fallen down into the Wolf Pit! Yes, they were quite near it. She remembered now that big white-birch tree stood right at the place where the brook tumbled over the edge and fell into it. Although she was dreadfully afraid of falling in herself, she went cautiously over to this tree, feeling her way with her foot to make sure she did not slip, and peered down into the cavernous gloom below. Yes, there was Molly's little face, just a white speck. The child was crying, sobbing, and holding up her arms to Betsy.

"Are you hurt, Molly?"

"No. I fell into a big snowbank, but I'm all wet and frozen and I want to get out! I want to get out!"

Betsy held on to the birch tree. Her head whirled. What *should* she do! "Look here, Molly," she called down, "I'm going to run back along to the right road and back to the house and get Uncle Henry. He'll come with a rope and get you out!"

At this Molly's crying rose to a frantic scream. "Oh, Betsy, don't leave me here alone! Don't! Don't! The wolves will get me! Betsy, *don't* leave me alone!" The child was wild with terror.

"But I *can't* get you out myself!" screamed back Betsy, crying herself. Her teeth were chattering with the cold.

"Don't go! Don't go!" came up from the darkness of the pit in a piteous howl. Betsy made a great effort and stopped crying. She sat down on a stone and tried to think. And this is what came into her mind as a guide: "What would Cousin Ann do if she were here? She wouldn't cry. She would *think* of something."

Betsy looked around her desperately. The first thing she saw was the big limb of a pine tree, broken off by the wind, which half lay and half slantingly stood up against a tree a little distance above the mouth of the pit. It had been there so long that the needles had dried and fallen off, and the skeleton of the branch with the broken stubs looked like . . . yes, it looked like a ladder! *That* was what Cousin Ann would have done!

"Wait a minute! Wait a minute, Molly!" she called wildly down the pit, warm all over in excitement. "Now listen. You go off there in a corner, where the ground makes a sort of roof. I'm going to throw down something you can climb up on, maybe."

"Ow! Ow, it'll hit me!" cried poor little Molly, more and more frightened. But she scrambled off under her shelter obediently, while Betsy struggled with the branch. It was so firmly imbedded in the snow that at first she could not budge it at all. But after she cleared that away and pried hard with the stick she was using as a lever she felt it give a little. She bore down with all her might, throwing her weight again and again on her lever, and finally felt the big branch move. After that it was easier, as its course was downhill over the snow to the mouth of the pit. Glowing and pushing, wet with perspiration, she slowly maneuvered it along to the edge, turned it squarely, gave it a great shove, and leaned over anxiously. Then she gave a great sigh of relief! Just as she had hoped, it went down sharp end first and stuck fast in the snow which had saved Molly from broken bones. She was so out of breath with her work that for a moment she could not speak. Then, "Molly, there! Now I guess you can climb up to where I can reach you."

Molly made a rush for any way out of her prison, and climbed, like the practiced squirrel that she was, up from one stub to another to the top of the branch. She was still below the edge of the pit there, but Betsy lay flat down on the snow and held out her hands. Molly took hold hard, and, digging her toes into the snow, slowly wormed her way up to the surface of the ground.

It was then, at that very moment, that Shep came bounding up to them, barking loudly, and after him Cousin Ann striding along in her rubber boots, with a lantern in her hand and a rather anxious look on her face.

She stopped short and looked at the two little girls, covered with snow, their faces flaming with excitement, and at the black hole gaping behind them. "I always *told* Father we ought to put a fence around that pit," she said in a matter-of-fact voice. "Someday a sheep's going to fall down there. Shep came along to the house without you, and we thought most likely you'd taken the wrong turn."

Betsy felt terribly aggrieved. She wanted to be petted and praised for her heroism. She wanted Cousin Ann to *realize* . . . oh, if Aunt Frances were only there, *she* would realize! . . .

"I fell down in the hole, and Betsy wanted to go and get Mr. Putney, but I wouldn't let her, and so she threw down a big branch and I climbed out," explained Molly, who, now that her danger was past, took Betsy's action quite as a matter of course.

"Oh, that was how it happened," said Cousin Ann. She looked down the hole and saw the big branch, and looked back and saw the long trail of crushed snow where Betsy had dragged it. "Well, now, that was quite a good idea for a little girl to have," she said briefly. "I guess you'll do to take care of Molly all right!"

She spoke in her usual voice and immediately drew the children after her, but Betsy's heart was singing joyfully as she trotted along clasping Cousin Ann's strong hand. Now she knew that Cousin Ann realized. . . . She trotted fast, smiling to herself in the darkness.

"What made you think of doing that?" asked Cousin Ann presently, as they approached the house.

"Why, I tried to think what *you* would have done if you'd been there," said Betsy.

"Oh!" said Cousin Ann. "Well . . ."

She didn't say another word, but Betsy, glancing up into her face as they stepped into the lighted room, saw an expression that made her give a little skip and hop of joy. She had *pleased* Cousin Ann.

That night, as she lay in her bed, her arm over Molly cuddled up warm beside her, she remembered, ever so faintly, as something of no importance, that she had failed in an examination that afternoon.

Betsy Starts a Sewing Society

Betsy and Molly had taken Deborah to school with them. Deborah was the old wooden doll with brown, painted curls. She had lain in a trunk almost ever since Aunt Abigail's childhood, because Cousin Ann had never cared for dolls when she was a little girl. At first Betsy had not dared to ask to see her, much less to play with her, but when Ellen, as she had promised, came over to Putney Farm that first Saturday she had said right out, as soon as she landed in the house, "Oh, Mrs. Putney, can't we play with Deborah?" And Aunt Abigail had answered: "Why, *yes*, of course! I *knew* there was something I've kept forgetting!" She went up with them herself to the cold attic and opened the little hair trunk under the eaves. There lay a doll, flat on her back, looking up at them brightly out of her blue eyes.

"Well, Debby dear," said Aunt Abigail, taking her up gently. "It's a good long time since you and I played under the lilac bushes, isn't it? I expect you've been pretty lonesome up here all these years. Never you mind, you'll have some good times again, now." She pulled down the doll's full, ruffled skirt, straightened the lace at the neck of her dress, and held her for a moment, looking down at her silently. You could tell by the way she spoke, by the way she touched Deborah, by the way she looked at her, that she had loved the doll dearly, and maybe still did, a little.

When she put Deborah into Betsy's arms, the child felt that she was receiving something precious, almost something alive. She and Ellen looked with delight at the yards and yards of picot-edged ribbon, sewed on by hand to the ruffles of the skirt, and lifted up the silk folds to admire the carefully made, full petticoats and frilly drawers, the pretty, soft old kid shoes and white stockings. Aunt Abigail looked at them with an absent smile on her lips, as though she were living over old scenes.

Finally, "It's too cold to play up here," she said, coming to herself with a long breath. "You'd better bring Deborah and the trunk down into the south room." She carried the doll, and Betsy and Ellen each took an end of the old trunk, no larger than a modern suitcase. They settled themselves on the big couch, back of the table with the lamp. Old Shep was on it, but Betsy coaxed him off by putting down some bones Cousin Ann had been saving for him. When he finished those and came back for the rest of his snooze, he found his place occupied by the little girls, sitting cross-legged, examining the contents of the trunk, all spread out around them. Shep sighed deeply and sat down with his nose resting on the couch near Betsy's knee, following their movements with his kind, dark eyes. Once in a while Betsy stopped hugging Deborah or exclaiming over a new dress long enough to pat Shep's head and fondle his ears. This was what he was waiting for, and every time she did it he wagged his tail thumpingly against the floor.

After that Deborah and her trunk were kept downstairs where Betsy could play with her. Often she was taken to school. You never heard of such a thing as taking a doll to school, did you? Well, I told you this was a queer, old-fashioned school. As a matter of fact, it was not only Betsy who took her doll to school; all the little girls did, whenever they felt like it. Miss Benton, the teacher, had a shelf for them in the entryway where the wraps were hung, and the dolls sat on it and waited patiently all through lessons. At recess time or noon each little mother snatched her own child and began to play. As soon as it grew warm enough to play outdoors without just racing around every minute to keep from freezing to death, the dolls and their mothers went out to a great pile of rocks at one end of the bare, stony field which was the playground. There they sat and played in the spring sunshine, warmer from day to day. There were a great many holes and shelves and pockets and little caves in the rocks which made lovely places for playing keep-house. Each little girl had her own particular cubbyholes and "rooms," and they "visited" their dolls back and forth all around the pile. And as they played they talked fast about all sorts of things, being little girls and not boys who just yelled and howled as they played ball or duck-on-a-rock or prisoner's goal, racing and running and wrestling noisily all around the rocks.

There was one child who neither played with the girls nor ran and whooped with the boys. This was little six-year-old 'Lias, one of the two boys in Molly's first grade. At recess time he generally hung about the school door by himself, looking moodily down and knocking the toe of his ragged, muddy shoe against a stone. The little girls were talking about him one day as they played. "My! Isn't that 'Lias Brewster the horridest-looking child!" said Eliza, who had the second grade all to herself, although Molly now read out of the second reader with her.

"Mercy, yes! So ragged!" said Anastasia Monahan, called Stashie for short. She was a big girl, fourteen years old, who was in the seventh grade.

"He doesn't look as if he *ever* combed his hair!" said Betsy. "It looks just like a wisp of old hay."

"And sometimes," little Molly proudly added her bit to the talk of the other girls, "he forgets to put on any stockings and just has his dreadful old shoes on over his dirty bare feet."

"I guess he hasn't *got* any stockings half the time," said big Stashie scornfully. "I guess his stepfather drinks 'em up."

"How *can* he drink up stockings?" asked Molly, opening her round eyes very wide.

"Shh! You mustn't ask. Little girls shouldn't know about such things, should they, Betsy?"

"No, *indeed*," said Betsy, looking mysterious. As a matter of fact, she herself had no idea what Stashie meant, but she looked wise and said nothing.

Some of the boys had squatted down near the rocks for a game of marbles now.

"Well, anyhow," said Molly resentfully, "I don't care what his stepfather does to his stockings. I wish 'Lias would wear 'em to school. And lots of times he hasn't anything on under those horrid old overalls either! I can see his bare skin through the torn places."

"I wish he didn't have to sit so near me," said Betsy complainingly. "He's *so* dirty."

"Well, I don't want him near *me*, either!" cried all the other little girls at once. Ralph glanced up at them frowning, from where he knelt with his middle finger crooked behind a marble ready for a shot. He looked as he always did, rough and half threatening. "You girls make me sick!" he said. He sent his marble straight to the mark, pocketed his opponent's, and stood up, scowling at the little mothers. "I guess if you had to live the way he does, you'd be dirty! Half the time he don't get anything to eat before he comes to school, and if my mother didn't put up some extra for him in my box he wouldn't get any lunch either. And then you go and jump on him!"

"Why doesn't his own mother put up his lunch?" Betsy challenged their critic.

"He hasn't got any mother. She's dead," said Ralph, turning away with his hands in his pockets. He yelled to the boys, "Come on, fellers, beat-cha to the bridge and back!" and was off, with the others racing at his heels.

"Well, anyhow, I don't care; he *is* dirty and horrid!" said Stashie emphatically, looking over at the drooping, battered little figure, leaning against the school door, listlessly kicking at a stone.

But Betsy did not say anything more just then.

The teacher, who "boarded 'round," was staying at Putney Farm at that time, and that evening, as they all sat around the lamp in the south room, Betsy looked up from her game of checkers with Uncle Henry and asked, "How can anybody drink up stockings?"

"Mercy, child! what are you talking about?" asked Aunt Abigail.

Betsy repeated what Anastasia Monahan had said, and was flattered by the rather startled attention given her by the grown-ups. "I didn't know that Bud Walker had taken to drinking again!" said Uncle Henry. "My! That's too bad!"

"Who takes care of that child anyhow, now that poor Susie is dead?" Aunt Abigail asked of everybody in general.

"Is he just living there *alone*, with that good-for-nothing stepfather? How do they get enough to *eat?*" said Cousin Ann, looking troubled.

Apparently Betsy's question had brought something half forgotten and altogether neglected into their minds. They talked for some time after that about 'Lias, the teacher confirming what Betsy and Stashie had said.

"And we sitting right here with plenty to eat and never raising a hand!" cried Aunt Abigail.

"How you *will* let things slip out of your mind!" said Cousin Ann remorsefully.

It struck Betsy vividly that 'Lias was not at all the one they blamed for his objectionable appearance. She felt quite ashamed to go on with the other things she and the little girls had said, and fell silent, pretending to be very much absorbed in her game of checkers.

"Do you know," said Aunt Abigail suddenly, as though an inspiration had just struck her, "I wouldn't be a bit surprised if that Elmore Pond might adopt 'Lias if he was gone at the right way."

"Who's Elmore Pond?" asked the schoolteacher.

"Why, you must have seen him—that great, big, red-faced, good-natured-looking man that comes through here twice a year, buying stock. He lives over Digby way, but his wife was a Hillsboro girl, Matey Pelham—an awfully nice girl she was, too. They never had any children, and Matey told me the last time she was back for a visit that she and her husband talked quite often about adopting a little boy. Seems that Mr. Pond has always wanted a little boy. He's such a nice man! 'Twould be a lovely home for a child."

"But goodness!" said the teacher. "Nobody would want to adopt such an awful-looking little ragamuffin as that 'Lias. He looks so meeching, too. I guess his stepfather is real mean to him, when he's been drinking, and it's got 'Lias so he hardly dares hold his head up."

The clock struck loudly. "Well, hear that!" said Cousin Ann. "Nine o'clock and the children not in bed! Molly's most asleep this minute. Trot along with you, Betsy! Trot along, Molly. And, Betsy, be sure Molly's nightgown is buttoned up all the way."

So it happened that, although the grown-ups were evidently going on to talk about 'Lias Brewster, Betsy heard no more of what they said.

She herself went on thinking about 'Lias while she was undressing and answering absently little Molly's chatter. She was thinking about him even after they had gone to bed, had put the light out, and were lying snuggled up to each other, back to front, their four legs, crooked at the same angle, fitting in together neatly like two spoons in a drawer. She was thinking about him when she woke up, and as soon as she could get hold of Cousin Ann she poured out a new plan. She had never been afraid of Cousin Ann since the evening Molly had fallen into the Wolf Pit and Betsy had seen that pleased smile on Cousin Ann's firm lips. "Cousin Ann, couldn't we girls at school get together and sew—you'd have to help us some—and make some nice, new clothes for little 'Lias Brewster, and fix him up so he'll look better, and maybe that Mr. Pond will like him and adopt him?"

Cousin Ann listened attentively and nodded her head. "Yes, I think that would be a good idea," she said. "We were thinking last night we ought to do something for him. If you'll make the clothes, Mother'll knit him some stockings and Father will get him some shoes. Mr. Pond never makes his spring trip till late May, so we'll have plenty of time."

Betsy was full of importance that day at school and at recess time got the girls together on the rocks and told them all about the plan. "Cousin Ann says she'll help us, and we can meet at our house every Saturday afternoon 'til we get them done. It'll be fun! Aunt Abigail telephoned down to the store right away, and Mr. Wilkins says he'll give the cloth if we'll make it up."

Betsy spoke very grandly of "making it up," although she had hardly held a needle in her life, and when the Saturday afternoon meetings began she was ashamed to see how much better Ellen and even Eliza could sew than she. To keep her end up, she was driven to practicing her stitches around the lamp in the evenings, with Aunt Abigail keeping an eye on her.

Cousin Ann supervised the sewing on Saturday afternoons and taught those of the little girls whose legs were long enough how to use the sewing machine. First they made a little pair of trousers out of an old gray woolen skirt of Aunt Abigail's. This was for practice, before they cut into the piece of new blue serge that the storekeeper had sent up. Cousin Ann showed them how to pin the pattern on the goods and they each cut out one piece. Those flat, queer-shaped pieces of cloth certainly did look less like a pair of trousers to Betsy than anything she had ever seen. Then one of the girls read aloud very slowly the mysterious-sounding directions from the wrapper of the pattern about how to put the pieces together. Cousin Ann helped here a little, particularly just as they were about to put the sections together wrong-side-up. Stashie, as the oldest, did the first basting, putting the notches together carefully, just as they read the instructions aloud, and there, all of a sudden, was a rough little sketch of a pair of knee trousers, without any hem or any waistband, of course, but just the two-legged, complicated shape they ought to be! It was like a miracle to Betsy! Cousin Ann helped them sew the seams on the machine, and they all turned to for the basting of the facings and the finishing. They each made one buttonhole. It was the first one Betsy had ever made, and when she got through she was as tired as though she had run all the way to school and back. Tired, but very proud, although when Cousin Ann inspected that buttonhole, she covered her face with her handkerchief for a minute, as though she were going to sneeze, although she didn't sneeze at all.

It took them two Saturdays to finish up that trial pair of trousers, and when they showed the result to Aunt Abigail she was delighted. "Well, to think of that being my old skirt!" she said, putting on her spectacles to examine the work. She did not laugh, either, when she saw those buttonholes, but she got up hastily and went into the next room, where they soon heard her coughing.

Then they made a little blouse out of some new blue gingham. Cousin Ann happened to have enough left over from a dress she was making. This thin material was ever so much easier to manage than the gray flannel, and they had the little garment done in no time, even to the buttons and buttonholes. When it came to making the buttonholes, Cousin Ann sat right down with each one and supervised every stitch. You may not be surprised to know that they were a great improvement over the first batch.

Then, making a great ceremony of it, they began on the store material, working twice a week now, because May was slipping along very fast, and Mr. Pond might be there at any time. They knew pretty well how to go ahead on this one, after the experience of their first pair, and Cousin Ann was not much needed, except as adviser in hard places. She sat there in the room with them, doing some sewing of her own, so quiet that half the time they forgot she was there. It was great fun, sewing all together and chatting as they sewed.

A good deal of the time they talked about how splendid it was of them to be so kind to little 'Lias.

"My! I don't believe most girls would put themselves out this way for a dirty little boy!" said Stashie, complacently.

"No, *indeed!*" chimed in Betsy. "It's just like a story, isn't it?—working and sacrificing for the poor!"

"I guess he'll thank us all right for sure!" said Ellen. "He'll never forget us as long as he lives, I don't suppose."

Betsy, her imagination fired by this suggestion, said, "I guess when he's grown up he'll be telling everybody about how, when he was so poor and ragged, Stashie Monahan and Ellen Peters and Elizabeth Ann . . ."

"And Eliza!" put in that little girl hastily, very much afraid she would not be given her due share of the glory.

Cousin Ann sewed, and listened, and said nothing.

Toward the end of May two little blouses, two pairs of trousers, two pairs of stockings, two sets of underwear (contributed by the teacher), and the pair of shoes Uncle Henry gave were ready. The little girls handled the pile of new garments with inexpressible pride, and debated just which way of bestowing them was sufficiently grand to be worthy the occasion. Betsy was for taking them to school and giving them to 'Lias one by one, so that each child could have her thanks separately. But Stashie wanted to take them to the house when 'Lias's stepfather would be there, and shame him by showing that little girls had had to do what he ought to have done.

Cousin Ann broke into the discussion by asking, in her quiet, firm voice, "What do you want 'Lias to know where the clothes come from?"

They had forgotten again that she was there, and turned around quickly to stare at her. Nobody could think of any answer to her very queer question. It had not occurred to anyone that there could *be* such a question.

Cousin Ann shifted her ground and asked another: "Why did you make these clothes, anyhow?"

They stared again, speechless. Why did she ask that? She knew why.

Finally little Molly said, in her honest, baby way, "Why, *you* know why, Miss Ann! So 'Lias Brewster will look nice, and Mr. Pond will maybe adopt him."

"Well," said Cousin Ann, "what has that got to do with 'Lias knowing who did it?"

"Why, he wouldn't know who to be grateful to," cried Betsy.

"Oh," said Cousin Ann. "Oh, I see. You didn't do it to help 'Lias. You did it to have him grateful to you. I see. Molly is such a little girl, it's no wonder she didn't really take in what you girls were up to." She nodded her head wisely, as though now she understood.

But if she did, little Molly certainly did not. She had not the least idea what everybody was talking about. She looked from one sober, downcast face to another rather anxiously. What was the matter?

Apparently nothing was really the matter, she decided, for after a minute's silence Miss Ann got up with her usual face of cheerful gravity, and said: "Don't you think you little girls ought to top off this last afternoon with a tea party? There's a new batch of cookies, and you can make yourselves some lemonade if you want to."

They had these refreshments out on the porch, in the sunshine, with their dolls for guests and a great deal of chatter for sauce. Nobody said another word about how to give the clothes to 'Lias, till, just as the girls were going away, Betsy said, walking along with the two older ones, "Say, don't you think it'd be fun to go some evening after dark and leave the clothes on 'Lias's doorstep, and knock and run away quick before anybody comes to the door?" She spoke in an uncertain voice and smoothed Deborah's carved wooden curls.

"Yes, I do!" said Ellen, not looking at Betsy but down at the weeds by the road. "I think it would be lots of fun!"

Little Molly, playing with Annie and Eliza, did not hear this; but she was allowed to go with the older girls on the great expedition.

It was a warm, dark evening in late May, with the frogs piping their sweet, high note, and the first of the fireflies wheeling over the wet meadows near the tumbledown house where 'Lias lived. The girls took turns in carrying the big paper-wrapped bundle, and stole along in the shadow of the trees, full of excitement, looking over their shoulders at nothing and pressing their hands over their mouths to keep back the giggles. There was, of course, no reason on earth why they should giggle, which is, of course, the reason why they did. If you've ever been a little girl you know about that.

One window of the small house was dimly lighted, they found, when they came in sight of it, and they thrilled with excitement and joyful alarm. Suppose 'Lias's dreadful step-father should come out and yell at them! They came forward on tiptoe, making a great deal of noise by stepping on twigs, rustling bushes, crackling gravel under their feet and doing all the other things that make such a noise at night and never do in the daytime. But nobody stirred inside the room with the lighted window. They crept forward and peeped cautiously inside . . . and stopped giggling. The dim light coming from a little kerosene lamp with a smoky chimney fell on a dismal, cluttered room, a bare, greasy wooden table, and two broken-backed chairs, with little 'Lias in one of them. He had fallen asleep with his head on his arms, his pinched, dirty, sad little figure showing in the light from the lamp. His feet dangled high above the floor in their broken, muddy shoes. One sleeve was torn to the shoulder. A piece of dry bread had slipped from his bony little hand and a tin dipper stood beside him on the bare table. Nobody else was in the room nor, evidently, in the darkened, empty, fireless house.

As long as she lives Betsy will never forget what she saw that night through that window. Her eyes grew very hot and her hands very cold. Her heart thumped hard. She reached for little Molly and gave her a great hug in the darkness. Suppose it were little Molly asleep there, all alone in the dirty, dismal house, with no supper and no-body to put her to bed. She found that Ellen, next her, was crying into the corner of her apron.

Nobody said a word. Stashie, who had the bundle,

walked around soberly to the front door, put it down, and knocked loudly. They all darted away noiselessly to the road, to the shadow of the trees, and waited until the door opened. A square of yellow light appeared, with 'Lias's figure, very small, at the bottom of it. They saw him stoop and pick up the bundle and go back into the house. Then they went quickly and silently back, separating at the crossroads with no good-night greetings.

Molly and Betsy began to climb the hill to Putney Farm. It was a very warm night for May, and little Molly began to puff for breath. "Let's sit down on this rock awhile and rest," she said.

They were halfway up the hill now. From the rock they could see the lights in the farmhouses scattered along the valley road and on the side of the mountain opposite them, like big stars fallen from the multitude above. Betsy lay down on the rock and looked up at the stars. After a silence little Molly's chirping voice said, "Oh, I thought you said we were going to march up to 'Lias in school and give him his clothes. Did you forget about that?"

Betsy gave a wriggle of shame as she remembered that plan. "No, we didn't forget it," she said. "We thought this would be a better way."

"But how'll 'Lias know who to thank?" asked Molly.

"That's no matter," said Betsy. Yes, it was Elizabeth-Ann-that-was who said that. And meant it, too. She was not even thinking of what she was saying. Between her and the stars, thick over her in the black, soft sky, she saw again that dirty, disordered room and the little boy, all alone, asleep with a piece of dry bread in his bony little fingers.

She looked hard and long at that picture, all the time seeing the quiet stars through it. And then she turned over and hid her face on the rock. She had said her "Now I lay me" every night since she could remember, but she had never prayed till she lay there with her face on the rock, saying over and over, "Oh, God, please, please, *please* make Mr. Pond adopt 'Lias."

The New Clothes Fail

The little girls went early to school the next day, eager for the first glimpse of 'Lias in his new clothes. They now quite enjoyed the mystery about who had made them, and were full of agreeable excitement as the little figure came down the road. He wore the gray trousers and the blue shirt; the trousers were a shade too long, the shirt a perfect fit. The girls gazed at him with pride as he came on the playground, walking briskly along in the new shoes, which were just the right size. He had been wearing all winter a pair of cast-off women's shoes.

From a distance he looked like another child. But as he came closer . . . oh! his face! his hair! his hands! his fingernails! The little fellow had evidently tried to live up to his beautiful new raiment, for his hair had been roughly put back from his face, and around his mouth and nose was a small area of almost clean skin, where he had made an attempt at washing his face. But he had made practically no impression on the layers of encrusted dirt, and the little girls looked at him ruefully. Mr. Pond would certainly never take a fancy to such a dreadfully grimy child! His new, clean clothes made him look all the worse, as though dirty on purpose!

The little girls retired to their rockpile and talked over their disappointment, Ralph and the other boys absorbed in a game of marbles near them. 'Lias had gone proudly into the schoolroom to show himself to Miss Benton.

It was the day before Decoration Day and a good deal of time was taken up with practicing on the recitations they were going to give at the Decoration Day exercises in the village. Several of the children from each school in the township were to speak pieces in the Town Hall. Betsy was to recite *Barbara Frietchie*, her first love in that school, but she droned it over with none of her usual pleasure, her eyes on little 'Lias's smiling face, so unconscious of its dinginess.

At noontime the boys disappeared down toward the swimming hole. They often took a swim at noon and nobody thought anything about it on that day. The little girls ate their lunch on their rock, mourning over the failure of their plans, and scheming ways to meet the new obstacle. Stashie suggested, "Couldn't your Aunt Abigail invite him up to your house for supper and then give him a bath afterward?" But Betsy, although she had never heard of treating a supper guest in this way, was sure that it was not possible. She shook her head sadly, her eyes on the far-off gleam of white where the boys jumped up and down in their swimming hole. That was not a good name for it, because there was only one part of it deep enough to swim in. Mostly it was a shallow bay in an arm of the river,

where the water was only up to a little boy's knees and
where there was almost no current. The sun beating down
on it made it quite warm, and even the first-graders' mothers allowed them to go in. They only jumped up and down
and squealed and splashed each other, but they enjoyed
that quite as much as Frank and Harry, the two seventh-
graders, enjoyed their swooping dives from the springboard
over the pool. They were late in getting back from the
river that day and Miss Benton had to ring her bell hard in
that direction before they came trooping up and clattered
into the schoolroom, where the girls already sat, their eyes
lowered virtuously to their books, with a prim air of self-
righteousness. *They* were never late!

Betsy was reciting her arithmetic. She was getting on
famously with that. Weeks ago, as soon as Miss Benton had
seen the confusion of the little girl's mind, the two had
settled down to a serious struggle with that subject. Miss
Benton had had Betsy recite all by herself, so she wouldn't
be flurried by the others; and to begin with had gone back,
back, back to bedrock, to things Betsy absolutely knew, to
the 2×2's and the 3×3's. And then, very cautiously, a
step at a time, they had advanced, stopping short whenever
Betsy felt a beginning of that bewildered "guessing" impulse which made her answer wildly at random.

After a while, in the dark night which arithmetic had
always been to her, Betsy began to make out a few definite
outlines, which were always there, facts which she knew to
be so without guessing from the expression of her teacher's
face. From that moment her progress had been rapid, one
sure fact hooking itself on to another, and another one on

to that. She attacked a page of problems now with a zest and self-confidence which made her arithmetic lessons among the most interesting hours at school. On that day she was standing up at the board, a piece of chalk in her hand, chewing her tongue and thinking hard how to find out the amount of wallpaper needed for a room 12 feet square with two doors and two windows in it, when her eyes fell on little 'Lias, bent over his reading book. She forgot her arithmetic, she forgot where she was. She stared and stared, till Ellen, catching the direction of her eyes, looked and stared too. Little 'Lias was *clean*, preternaturally, almost wetly clean. His face was clean and shining, his ears shone pink and fair, his hands were absolutely spotless, even his hay-colored hair was clean and, still damp, brushed flatly back till it shone in the sun. Betsy blinked her eyes a great many times, thinking she must be dreaming, but every time she opened them there was 'Lias, looking white and polished like a new willow whistle.

Somebody poked her hard in the ribs. She started and, turning, saw Ralph, who was doing a sum beside her on the board, scowling at her under his black brows. "Quit gawking at 'Lias," he said under his breath. "You make me tired!" Something conscious and shame-faced in his manner made Betsy understand at once what had happened. Ralph had taken 'Lias down to the little boys' wading place and had washed him all over. She remembered now that they had a piece of yellow soap there.

Her face broke into a radiant smile and she began to say something to Ralph about how nice that was of him, but he frowned again and said, crossly, "Aw, cut it out! Look at what you've done there! If I couldn't 9×8 and get it right!"

"How queer boys are!" thought Betsy, erasing her mistake and putting down the right answer. But she did not try to speak to Ralph again about 'Lias, not even after school, when she saw 'Lias going home with a new cap on his head which she recognized as Ralph's. She just looked at Ralph's bare head, and smiled her eyes at him, keeping the rest of her face sober, the way Cousin Ann did. For a minute Ralph almost smiled back. At least he looked quite friendly. They stepped along toward home together, the first time Ralph had ever condescended to walk beside a girl.

"We got a new colt," he said.

"Have you?" she said. "What color?"

"Black, with a white star, and they're going to let me ride him when he's old enough."

"My! Won't that be nice!" said Betsy.

And all the time they were both thinking of little 'Lias with his new clothes and his sweet, thin face shining with cleanliness.

"Do you like spruce gum?" asked Ralph.

"Oh. I *love* gum!" said Betsy.

"Well, I'll bring you down a chunk tomorrow, if I don't forget it," said Ralph, turning off at the crossroads.

They had not mentioned 'Lias at all.

The next day they were to have school only in the morning. In the afternoon they were to go in a big hay wagon down to the village to the "exercises." 'Lias came to school in his new blue serge trousers and his white blouse.

The little girls gloated over his appearance, and hung around him, for who was to "visit school" that morning but Mr. Pond himself! Cousin Ann had arranged it somehow. It took Cousin Ann to fix things! During recess, as they were playing still-pond-no-more-moving on the playground, Mr. Pond and Uncle Henry drew up to the edge of the playground, stopped their horse, and, talking and laughing together, watched the children at play. Betsy looked hard at the big, burly, kind-faced man with the smiling eyes and the hearty laugh, and decided that he would "do" perfectly for 'Lias. But what she decided was to have little importance, apparently, for after all he would not get out of the wagon, but said he'd have to drive right on to the village. Just like that, with no excuse other than a careless glance at his watch. No, he guessed he wouldn't have time, this morning, he said. Betsy cast an imploring look up into Uncle Henry's face, but evidently he felt himself quite helpless, too. Oh, if only Cousin Ann had come! *She* would have marched him into the schoolhouse double quick. But Uncle Henry was not Cousin Ann, and though Betsy saw him, as they drove away, conscientiously point out little 'Lias, resplendent and shining, Mr. Pond only nodded absently, as though he were thinking of something else.

Betsy could have cried with disappointment; but she and the other girls, putting their heads together for comfort, told each other that there was time enough yet. Mr. Pond would not leave town till tomorrow. Perhaps . . . there was still some hope.

But that afternoon even this last hope was dashed. As

they gathered at the schoolhouse, the girls fresh and crisp in their newly starched dresses, with red or blue hair ribbons, the boys very self-conscious in their dark suits, clean collars, new caps (all but Ralph), and blacked shoes, there was no little 'Lias. They waited and waited, but there was no sign of him. Finally Uncle Henry, who was to drive the straw ride down to town, looked at his watch, gathered up the reins, and said they would be late if they didn't start right away. Maybe 'Lias had had a chance to ride in with somebody else.

They all piled in, the horses stepped off, the wheels grated on the stones. And just at that moment a dismal sound of sobbing reached them from the woodshed back of the schoolhouse. The children tumbled out as fast as they had tumbled in, and ran back, Betsy and Ralph at their head. There in the woodshed was little 'Lias, huddled in the corner behind some wood, crying and crying and crying, digging his fists into his eyes, his face all smeared with tears and dirt. And he was dressed again in his filthy, torn old overalls and ragged shirt. His poor little bare feet shone with a piteous cleanliness in that dark place.

"What's the matter? What's the matter?" the children asked him all at once. He flung himself on Ralph, burying his face in the other boy's coat, and sobbed out some disjointed story which only Ralph could hear . . . and then as last and final climax of the disaster, who should come looking over the shoulders of the children but Uncle Henry *and Mr. Pond!* And 'Lias all ragged and dirty again! Betsy sat down weakly on a pile of wood, discouraged. What was the use of anything!

"What's the matter?" asked the two men together.

Ralph turned, with an angry toss of his dark head, and told them bitterly, over the heads of the children: "He just had some decent clothes. . . . First ones he's *ever* had! And he was lotting on going to the exercises in the Town Hall. And that darned old skunk of a stepfather has gone and taken 'em and sold 'em to get whisky. I'd like to *kill* him!"

Betsy could have flung her arms around Ralph, he looked so exactly the way she felt. "Yes, he *is* a darned old skunk!" she said to herself, rejoicing in the bad words she did not know before. It *took* bad words to qualify what had happened.

She saw an electric spark pass from Ralph's blazing eyes to Mr. Pond's broad face, now grim and fierce. She saw Mr. Pond step forward, brushing the children out of his way, like a giant among dwarfs. She saw him stoop and pick little 'Lias up in his great, strong arms, and, holding him close, stride furiously out of the woodshed, across the playground to the buggy which was waiting for him.

"He'll go to the exercises all right!" he called back over his shoulder in a great roar. "He'll go if I have to buy out the whole town to get him an outfit! And that whelp won't get these clothes, either; you hear me say so!"

He sprang into the buggy and, holding 'Lias on his lap, took up the reins and drove rapidly forward.

They saw 'Lias again, entering the Town Hall, holding fast to Mr. Pond's hand. He was magnificent in a whole suit of store clothes, coat and all, and he wore white stockings and neat, low shoes, like a city child!

They saw him later, up on the platform, squeaking out his little patriotic poem, his eyes, shining like stars, fixed on one broad, smiling face in the audience. When he finished he was overcome with shyness by the applause, and for a moment forgot to turn and leave the platform. He hung his head, and, looking out from under his eyebrows, gave a quaint, shy smile at the audience. Betsy saw Mr. Pond's great smile waver and grow dim. His eyes filled so full that he had to take out his handkerchief and blow his nose loudly.

They saw little 'Lias once more, for the last time. Mr. Pond's buggy drove rapidly past their slow-moving hay wagon, Mr. Pond holding the reins masterfully in one hand. Beside him, very close, sat 'Lias with his lap full of toys, oh, *full*—like Christmas! In that fleeting glimpse they saw a toy train, a stuffed dog, a candy box, a pile of picture books, tops, paper bags, and even the swinging crane of the big mechanical toy dredge that everybody said the store-keeper could never sell to anybody because it cost so much!

As they passed swiftly, 'Lias looked out at them and waved his hand flutteringly. His other hand was tightly clasped in Mr. Pond's big one. He was smiling at them all. His eyes looked dazed and radiant. He turned his head as the buggy flashed by to call out, in a shrill, exulting shout, "Good-by! Good-by! I'm going to live with . . ." They could hear no more. He was gone, only his little hand still waving at them over the back of the buggy seat.

Betsy drew a long, long breath. She found that Ralph was looking at her. For a moment, she couldn't think what made him look so different. Then she saw that he was smiling. She had never seen him smile before. He smiled at her as though he were sure she would understand, and never said a word. Betsy looked forward again and saw the gleaming buggy vanishing over the hill in front of them. She smiled back at Ralph silently.

Not a thing had happened the way she had planned, no, not a single thing! But it seemed to her she had never been so happy in her life.

Betsy Has
a Birthday

Betsy's birthday was the ninth day of September, and the Necronsett Valley Fair is always held from the eighth to the twelfth. So it was decided that Betsy should celebrate her birthday by going up to Woodford, where the Fair was held. The Putneys weren't going that year, but the people on the next farm, the Wendells, said they could make room in their surrey for the two little girls, for, of course, Molly was going, too. In fact, she said the Fair was held partly to celebrate her being six years old. This would happen on the seventeenth of October. Molly insisted that that was *plenty* close enough to the ninth of September to be celebrated then. This made Betsy feel like laughing, but observing that the Putneys only looked at each other with the faintest possible quirk in the corners of their serious mouths, she understood that they were afraid that Molly's feelings might be hurt if they laughed out loud. So Betsy tried to curve her young lips to the same kind and secret mirth.

And, I can't tell you why, this effort not to hurt Molly's feelings made her have a perfect spasm of love for Molly. She threw herself on her and gave her a great hug that tipped them both over on the couch on top of Shep, who stopped snoring with his great gurgling snort, wriggled out from under them, and stood with laughing eyes and wagging tail, looking at them as they rolled and giggled among the pillows.

"What dress are you going to wear to the Fair, Betsy?" asked Cousin Ann. "And we must decide about Molly's, too."

This stopped their rough-and-tumble fun in short order, and they applied themselves to serious questions.

When the great day arrived and the surrey drove away from the Wendells' gate, Betsy was in a fresh pink and white gingham which she had helped Cousin Ann make, and plump Molly looked like something good to eat in a crisp white dimity, one of Betsy's old dresses, with a deep hem taken in to make it short enough for the tiny butterball. Because it was Betsy's birthday, she sat on the front seat with Mr. Wendell, and part of the time, when there were not too many teams on the road, she drove, herself. Mrs. Wendell and her sister filled the back seat solidly full from side to side and made one continuous soft lap on which Molly happily perched, her eyes shining, her round cheeks red with joyful excitement. Betsy looked back at her several times and thought how nice Molly looked. She had, of course, little idea how she herself looked because the mirrors at Putney Farm were all small and high up, and anyhow they were so old and greenish that they made everybody look very queer-colored. You looked in them to see if your hair was smooth, and that was about all you could stand.

So it was a great surprise to Betsy later in the morning, as she and Molly wandered hand-in-hand through the wonders of Industrial Hall, to catch sight of Molly in a full-length mirror as clear as water. She was almost startled to see how faithfully reflected were the yellow of the little girl's curls, the clear pink and white of her face, and the blue of her soft eyes. An older girl was reflected there also, near Molly, a dark-eyed, red-cheeked, sturdy girl, standing straight on two strong legs, holding her head high and free, her dark eyes looking out brightly from her tanned face. For an instant Betsy gazed into those clear eyes and then . . . why, gracious goodness! That was herself she was looking at! How changed she was! How very, very different she looked from the last time she had seen herself in a big mirror! She remembered it well—out shopping with Aunt Frances in a department store, she had caught sight of a pale child with a thin neck and spindling legs half-hidden in the folds of Aunt Frances's skirts. But she didn't look even like the sister of this browned, muscular, upstanding child who held Molly's hand so firmly.

All this came into her mind and went out again in a moment, for Molly caught sight of a big doll in the next aisle and they hurried over to inspect her clothing. The mirror was forgotten in the many exciting sights and sounds and smells of their first county fair.

The two little girls were to wander about as they pleased until noon, when they were to meet the Wendells in the shadow of Industrial Hall and eat their picnic lunch together. The two parties arrived together from different directions, having seen very different sides of the Fair. The children were full of the merry-go-rounds, the balloon-seller, the toy-vendors, and the popcorn stands, while the Wendells exchanged views on the shortness of a hog's legs, the dip in a cow's back, and the thickness of a sheep's wool. The Wendells, it seemed, had met some cousins they didn't expect to see, who, not knowing about Betsy and Molly, had hoped that they might ride home with the Wendells.

"Don't you suppose," Mrs. Wendell asked Betsy, "that you and Molly could go home with the Vaughans? They're here in their big wagon. You could sit on the floor with the Vaughan children."

Betsy and Molly thought this would be fun, and agreed enthusiastically.

"All right, then," said Mrs. Wendell. She called to a young man who stood inside the building, near an open window: "Oh, Frank, Will Vaughan is going to be in your booth this afternoon, isn't he?"

"Yes, ma'am," said the young man. "His turn is from two to four."

"Well, you tell him, will you, that the two little girls who live at Putney Farm are going to go home with them. They can sit on the bottom of the wagon with the Vaughan young ones."

"Yes, ma'am," said the young man, with a noticeable lack of interest in how Betsy and Molly got home.

"Now, Betsy," said Mrs. Wendell, "you go round to that

booth at two and ask Will Vaughan what time they're going to start and where their wagon is, and then you be sure
not to keep them waiting a minute."

"No, I won't," said Betsy. "I'll be sure to be there on
time."

She and Molly still had twenty cents to spend out of the
forty they had brought with them, twenty-five earned by
berry-picking and fifteen a present from Uncle Henry.
They now put their heads together to see how they could
make the best possible use of their four nickels. Cousin
Ann had put no restrictions whatever on them, saying they
could buy any sort of truck or rubbish they could find,
except the pink lemonade. She said she had been told the
vendors washed their glasses in that, and their hands, and
for all she knew their faces. Betsy was for merry-go-rounds,
but Molly yearned for a big red balloon; and while they
were buying that a man came by with toy dogs, little brown
dogs with curled-wire tails. He called out that they would
bark when you pulled their tails, and seeing the little girls
looking at him he pulled the tail of the one he held. It gave
forth a fine loud yelp, just like Shep when his tail got
stepped on. Betsy bought one, all done up neatly in a box
tied with blue string. She thought it a great bargain to get a
dog who would bark for five cents. (Later on, when they
undid the string and opened the box, they found the dog
had one leg broken off and wouldn't make the faintest
squeak when his tail was pulled; but that is the sort of
thing you must expect to have happen to you at a county
fair.)

Now they had ten cents left and they decided to have a

ride apiece on the merry-go-round. But, glancing up at the
clock face in the tower over Agricultural Hall, Betsy noticed it was half-past two and she decided to go first to the
booth where Will Vaughan was to be and find out what
time they would start for home. She found the booth with
no difficulty, but William Vaughan was not in it. Nor was
the young man she had seen before. There was a new one,
a strange one, a careless, whistling young man, with very
bright socks, and striped cuffs. He said, in answer to Betsy's
inquiry: "Vaughan? Will Vaughan? Never heard the
name," and immediately went on whistling and looking up
and down the aisle over the heads of the little girls, who
stood gazing up at him with very wide, startled eyes. An
older man leaned over from the next booth and said: "Will
Vaughan? He from Hillsboro? Well, I heard somebody say
those Hillsboro Vaughans had word one of their cows was
awful sick, and they had to start right home that minute."

Betsy came to herself out of her momentary daze and
snatched Molly's hand. "Hurry! quick! We must find the
Wendells before they get away!"

In her agitation (for she was really very much frightened) she forgot how easily terrified little Molly was. Her
alarm instantly sent the child into a panic. "Oh, Betsy!
Betsy! What will we do!" she gasped, as Betsy pulled her
along the aisle and out of the door.

"Oh, the Wendells can't be gone yet," said Betsy reassur-
ingly, though she was not at all sure she was telling the
truth. She ran as fast as she could drag Molly's fat legs, to
the horse shed where Mr. Wendell had tied his horses and
left the surrey. The horse shed was empty, quite empty.

Betsy stopped short and stood still, her heart seeming to be up in her throat so that she could hardly breathe. After all, she was only ten that day, you must remember. Molly began to cry loudly, hiding her weeping face in Betsy's dress. "What will we do, Betsy! What can we *do!*" she wailed.

Betsy did not answer. She did not know what they *would* do! They were eight miles from Putney Farm, far too much for Molly to walk, and anyhow neither of them knew the way. They had only ten cents left, and nothing to eat. And the only people they knew in all that throng of strangers had gone back to Hillsboro.

"What will we do, Betsy?" Molly kept on crying out, horrified by Betsy's silence.

The other child's head swam. She tried again the formula which had helped her when Molly fell into the Wolf Pit, and asked herself, desperately, "What would Cousin Ann do if she were here?" But that did not help her much now, because she could not possibly imagine what Cousin Ann would do under such appalling circumstances. Yes, one thing Cousin Ann would be sure to do, of course; she would quiet Molly first of all.

At this thought Betsy sat down on the ground and took the panic-stricken little girl into her lap, wiping away the tears and saying, stoutly, "Now, Molly, stop crying this minute. I'll take care of you, of course. I'll get you home all right."

"How'll you ever do it?" sobbed Molly. "Everybody's gone and left us. We can't walk!"

"Never you mind how," said Betsy, trying to be facetious

and mock-mysterious, though her own underlip was quivering a little. "That's my surprise party for you. Just you wait. Now come on back to that booth. Maybe Will Vaughan didn't go home with his folks."

She had very little hope of this, and only went back there because it seemed to her a little less dauntingly strange than every other spot in the howling wilderness about her; for all at once the Fair, which had seemed so lively and cheerful and gay before, seemed now a frightening, noisy place, full of hurried strangers who came and went their own ways, with not a glance out of their hard eyes for two little girls stranded far from home.

The bright-colored young man was no better when they found him again. He stopped his whistling only long enough to say, "Nope, no Will Vaughan anywhere around these diggings yet."

"We were going home with the Vaughans," murmured Betsy, in a low tone, hoping for some help from him.

"Looks as though you'd better go home on the cars," advised the young man casually. He smoothed his black hair back straighter than ever from his forehead and looked over their heads.

"How much does it cost to go to Hillsboro on the cars?" asked Betsy with a sinking heart.

"You'll have to ask somebody else about that," said the young man. "What I don't know about this rube state! I never was in it before." He spoke as though he were proud of the fact.

Betsy turned and went over to the older man who had told them about the Vaughans.

Molly trotted at her heels, quite comforted, now that Betsy was talking so competently to grown-ups. She did not hear what they said, nor try to. Now that Betsy's voice sounded all right she had no more fears. Betsy would manage somehow. She heard Betsy's voice again talking to the other man, but she was busy looking at an exhibit of beautiful jelly glasses, and paid no attention. Then Betsy led her away again out of doors, where everybody was walking back and forth under the bright September sky, blowing on horns, waving plumes of brilliant tissue paper, tickling each other with peacock feathers, and eating popcorn and candy out of paper bags.

That reminded Molly that they had ten cents yet. "Oh, Betsy," she proposed, "let's take a nickel of our money for some popcorn."

She was startled by Betsy's fierce sudden clutch at their little purse and by the quaver in her voice as she answered: "No, no, Molly. We've got to save every cent of that. I've found out it costs thirty cents for us both to go home to Hillsboro on the train. The last one goes at six o'clock."

"We haven't got but ten," said Molly.

Betsy looked at her silently for a moment and then burst out, "I'll earn the rest! I'll earn it somehow! I'll have to! There isn't any other way!"

"All right," said Molly quaintly, not seeing anything unusual in this. "You can, if you want to. I'll wait for you here."

"No, you won't!" cried Betsy, who had quite enough of trying to meet people in a crowd. "No, you won't! You just follow me every minute! I don't want you out of my sight!"

They began to move forward now, Betsy's eyes wildly roving from one place to another. How *could* a little girl earn money at a county fair! She was horribly afraid to go up and speak to a stranger, and yet how else could she begin?

"Here, Molly, you wait here," she said. "Don't you budge till I come back."

But alas! Molly had only a moment to wait that time, for the man who was selling lemonade answered Betsy's shy question with a stare and a curt, "Lord, no! What could a young one like you do for me?"

The little girls wandered on, Molly calm and expectant, confident in Betsy; Betsy with a dry mouth and a gone feeling. They were passing by a big shed-like building now, where a large sign proclaimed that the Woodford Ladies' Aid Society would serve a hot chicken dinner for thirty-five cents. Of course the sign was not accurate, for at half-past three, almost four, the chicken dinner had long ago been all eaten and in place of the diners was a group of weary women moving languidly about or standing saggingly by a great table piled with dirty dishes. Betsy paused here, meditated a moment, and went in rapidly so that her courage would not evaporate.

The woman with gray hair looked down at her a little impatiently and said, "Dinner's all over."

"I didn't come for dinner," said Betsy, swallowing hard. "I came to see if you wouldn't hire me to wash your dishes. I'll do them for twenty-five cents."

The woman laughed, looked from little Betsy to the great pile of dishes, and said, turning away, "Mercy, child, if you washed from now till morning, you wouldn't make a hole in what we've got to do."

Betsy heard her say to the other women, "Some young one wanting more money for the sideshows."

Now, now was the moment to remember what Cousin Ann would have done. She would certainly not have shaken all over with hurt feelings nor have allowed the tears to come stingingly to her eyes. So Betsy sternly made herself stop doing these things. And Cousin Ann wouldn't have given way to the dreadful sinking feeling of discouragement, but would have gone right on to the next place. So, although Betsy felt like nothing so much as crooking her elbow over her face and crying as hard as she could cry, she stiffened her back, took Molly's hand again, and stepped out, heartsick within but very steady (although rather pale) without.

She and Molly walked along in the crowd again, Molly laughing and pointing out the pranks and antics of the young people, who were feeling livelier than ever as the afternoon wore on. Betsy looked at them grimly with unseeing eyes. It was four o'clock. The last train for Hillsboro left in two hours and she was no nearer having the price of the tickets. She stopped for a moment to get her breath; for, although they were walking slowly, she kept feeling breathless and choked. It occurred to her that if ever a little girl had had a more horrible birthday she never heard of one!

"Oh, I wish I could, Dan!" said a young voice near her. "But honest! Momma'd just eat me up alive if I left the booth for a minute!"

Betsy turned quickly. A very pretty girl with yellow hair and blue eyes (she looked as Molly might when she was grown up) was leaning over the edge of a little canvas-covered booth, the sign of which announced that home-made doughnuts and soft drinks were for sale there. A young man, very flushed and gay, was pulling at the girl's blue gingham sleeve. "Oh, come on, Annie. Just one turn! The floor's just right. You can keep an eye on the booth from the hall! Nobody's going to run away with the old thing anyhow!"

"Honest, I'd love to! But I got a great lot of dishes to wash, too! You know Momma!" She looked longingly toward the open-air dancing floor, out from which just then floated a burst of brassy music.

"Oh, *please!*" said a small voice. "I'll do it for twenty cents."

Betsy stood by the girl's elbow, quivering earnestness.

"Do what, kiddie?" asked the girl in good-natured surprise.

"Everything!" said Betsy, compendiously. "Everything! Wash the dishes, tend the booth; *you* can go dance! I'll do it for twenty cents."

The eyes of the girl and the man met. "My! Aren't we up and coming!" said the man. "You're most as big as a pint cup, aren't you?" he said to Betsy.

The little girl flushed—she detested being laughed at—but she looked straight into the laughing eyes. "I'm ten years old today," she said, "and I can wash dishes as well as anybody." She spoke with dignity.

The young man burst out into a great laugh.

"Great kid, what?" he said to the girl, and then, "Say, Annie, why not? Your mother won't be here for an hour. The kid can keep folks from walking off with the stuff and . . ."

"I'll do the dishes, too," repeated Betsy, trying hard not to mind being laughed at, and keeping her eyes fixed steadily on the tickets to Hillsboro.

"Well, by gosh," said the young man, laughing. "Here's our chance, Annie, for fair! Come along!"

The girl laughed, too, out of high spirits. "Wouldn't Momma be crazy!" she said hilariously. "But she'll never know. Here, you cute kid, here's my apron." She took off her long apron and tied it around Betsy's neck. "There's the soap, there's the table. Stack the dishes up on that counter."

She was out of the little gate in the counter in a twinkling, just as Molly, in answer to a beckoning gesture from Betsy, came in. "Hello, there's another one!" said the gay young man, gayer and gayer. "Hello, button! What you going to do? I suppose when they try to crack the safe you'll run at them and bark and drive them away!"

Molly opened her sweet, blue eyes wide, not understanding a single word. The girl laughed, swooped back, gave Molly a kiss, and disappeared, running side by side with the young man toward the dance hall.

Betsy mounted on a soap box and began joyfully to wash the dishes. She had never thought that ever in her life would she simply *love* to wash dishes beyond anything else! But it was so. Her relief was so great that she could have kissed the coarse, thick plates and glasses as she washed them.

"It's all right, Molly; it's all right!" she quavered exultantly to Molly over her shoulder. But as Molly had not (from the moment Betsy took command) suspected that it was not all right, she only nodded and asked if she might sit up on a barrel where she could watch the crowd go by.

"I guess you could. I don't know why *not*," said Betsy doubtfully. She lifted her up and went back to her dishes. Never were dishes washed better!

"Two doughnuts, please," said a man's voice behind her.

Oh, mercy, there was somebody come to buy! Whatever should she do? She came forward intending to say that the owner of the booth was away and she didn't know anything about . . . but the man laid down a nickel, took two doughnuts, and turned away. Betsy gasped and looked at the home-made sign stuck into the big pan of doughnuts. Sure enough, it read "2 for 5." She put the nickel up on a shelf and went back to her dishwashing. Selling things wasn't so hard, she reflected.

Now that she saw a way out, she began to find some fun being behind a counter instead of in front. When a woman with two little boys approached, she came forward to wait on her, feeling important. "Two for five," she said in a businesslike tone. The woman put down a dime, took up four doughnuts, divided them between her sons, and departed.

"My!" said Molly, looking admiringly at Betsy's coolness. Betsy went back to her dishes, stepping high.

"Oh, Betsy, see! The pig! The big ox!" cried Molly now,

looking from her coign of vantage down the wide, grass-grown lane between the booths.

Betsy craned her head around over her shoulder, con-tinuing conscientiously to wash and wipe the dishes. The prize stock was being paraded around the Fair; the huge prize ox, his shining horns tipped with blue rosettes; the prize cows, with wreaths around their necks; the prize horses, four or five of them as glossy as satin, curving their bright, strong necks and stepping as though on eggs, their manes and tails braided with bright ribbon; and then, "Oh, Betsy, *look* at the pig!" screamed Molly again—the smaller animals, the sheep, the calves, the colts, and the pig, which waddled along with portly dignity.

Betsy looked as well as she could over her shoulder . . . and in years to come she could shut her eyes and see again in every detail that procession under the golden September light.

But she looked anxiously at the clock. It was nearing five. Oh, suppose the girl forgot and danced too long!

"Two bottles of ginger ale and half a dozen doughnuts," said a man with a woman and three children.

Betsy looked feverishly among the bottles ranged on the counter, selected two marked ginger ale, and glared at their corrugated tin stoppers. How *did* you get them open?

"Here's your opener," said the man, "if that's what you're looking for. You get the glasses and I'll open the bottles. We're in kind of a hurry. Got to catch a train."

Well, they were not the only people who had to catch a train, Betsy thought sadly. They drank in gulps and de-parted, cramming doughnuts into their mouths. Betsy

wished that the girl would come back. She was now almost
sure that she had forgotten and would dance till nightfall.
But there, there she came, running along, as light-footed
after an hour's dancing as when she had left the booth.

"Here you are, kid," said the young man, producing a
quarter. "We've had the time of our young lives, thanks to
you."

Betsy gave him back one of the nickels that remained to
her, but he refused it.

"No, keep the change," he said royally. "It was worth
it."

"Then I'll buy two doughnuts with my extra nickel,"
said Betsy.

"No, you won't," said the girl. "You'll take all you want
for nothing . . . Momma'll never miss 'em. What you sell
here has got to be fresh every day anyhow. Here, hold out
your hands, both of you."

"Some people came and bought things," said Betsy, hap-
pening to remember as she and Molly turned away. "The
money is on that shelf."

"Well, *now*," said the girl, "if she didn't take hold and
sell things! Say . . ."—she ran after Betsy and gave her a
hug—"you smart young one, I wish't I had a little sister just
like you!"

Molly and Betsy hurried along out of the gate into the
main street of the town and down to the station. Molly was
eating doughnuts as she went. They were both quite hungry by this time, but Betsy could not think of eating till she
had those tickets in her hand.

She pushed her quarter and a nickel into the ticket

seller's window and said "Hillsboro" in as confident a tone as she could, but when the precious bits of paper were pushed out at her and she actually held them, her knees shook under her and she had to go and sit down on the bench.

"My! Aren't these doughnuts good?" said Molly. "I never in my life had *enough* doughnuts before!"

Betsy drew a long breath and began rather languidly to eat one herself; she felt, all of a sudden, very, very tired.

She was tireder still when they got out of the train at Hillsboro Station and started wearily up the road toward Putney Farm. Two miles lay before them, two miles which they had often walked before, but never after such a day as now lay in back of them. Molly dragged her feet as she walked and hung heavily on Betsy's hand. Betsy plodded along, her head hanging, her eyes gritty with sleepiness. A light buggy spun around the turn of the road behind them, the single horse trotting fast as though the driver were in a hurry, the wheels rattling smartly on the hard road. The little girls drew out to one side and stood waiting till the road should be free again. When he saw them the driver pulled the horse back so quickly it stood almost straight up. He peered at them through the twilight and then with a loud shout sprang over the side of the buggy.

It was Uncle Henry—oh, goody, it was Uncle Henry come to meet them! They wouldn't have to walk any further!

But what was the matter with Uncle Henry? He ran up to them, exclaiming, "Are ye all right? Are ye all right?" He stooped over and felt of them desperately as though he expected them to be broken somewhere. And Betsy could feel that his old hands were shaking, that he was trembling all over. When she said, "Why, yes, Uncle Henry, we're all right. We came home on the cars," Uncle Henry leaned up against the fence as though he couldn't stand up. He took off his hat and wiped his forehead and he said—it didn't seem as though it could be Uncle Henry talking, he sounded so excited—"Well, well—well, by gosh! My! Well, by thunder! Now! And so here ye are! And you're all right! *Well!*"

He couldn't seem to stop exclaiming, and you can't imagine anything stranger than an Uncle Henry who couldn't stop exclaiming.

After they all got into the buggy he quieted down a little and said, "Thunderation! But we've had a scare! When the Wendells came back with their cousins early this afternoon, they said you were coming with the Vaughans. And then when you didn't come and *didn't* come, we telephoned to the Vaughans, and they said they hadn't seen hide nor hair of ye, and didn't even know you were *to* the Fair at all! I tell you, your Aunt Abigail and I had an awful turn! Ann and I hitched up quicker'n scat and she put right out with Prince up toward Woodford and I took Jessie down this way; thought maybe I'd get trace of ye somewhere here. Well, land!" He wiped his forehead again. "Wa'n't I glad to see you standin' there . . . get along, Jess! I want to get the news to Abigail soon as I can!"

"Now tell me what in thunder *did* happen to you!"

Betsy began at the beginning and told straight through, interrupted at first by indignant comments from Uncle

Henry, who was outraged by the Wendells' loose wearing of their responsibility for the children. But as she went on he quieted down to a closely attentive silence, interrupting only to keep Jess at her top speed.

Now that it was all safely over, Betsy thought her story quite an interesting one, and she omitted no detail, although she wondered once or twice if perhaps Uncle Henry were listening to her, he kept so still. "And so I bought the tickets and we got home," she ended, adding, "Oh, Uncle Henry, you ought to have seen the prize pig! He was *too* funny!"

They turned into the Putney yard now and saw Aunt Abigail's bulky form on the porch.

"Got 'em, Abby! All right! No harm done!" shouted Uncle Henry.

Aunt Abigail turned without a word and went back into the house. When the little girls dragged their weary legs in they found her quietly setting out some supper for them on the table, but she was wiping away with her apron the joyful tears which ran down her cheeks, such pale cheeks! It seemed so strange to see rosy Aunt Abigail with a face as white as paper.

"Well, I'm glad to see ye," she told them soberly. "Sit right down and have some hot milk. I had some all ready."

The telephone rang, she went into the next room, and they heard her saying, in an unsteady voice: "All right, Ann. They're here. Your father just brought them in. I haven't had time to hear about what happened yet. But they're all right. You'd better come home."

"That's your Cousin Ann telephoning from the Marshalls'."

She herself went and sat down heavily, and when Uncle Henry came in a few minutes later she asked him in a rather weak voice for the ammonia bottle. He rushed for it, got her a fan and a drink of cold water, and hung over her anxiously till the color began to come back into her pale face. "I know just how you feel, Mother," he said sympathetically. "When I saw 'em standin' there by the roadside I felt as though somebody had hit me a clip right in the pit of the stomach."

The little girls ate their supper in a tired daze, not paying any attention to what the grownups were saying, until rapid hoofs clicked on the stones outside and Cousin Ann came in quickly, her black eyes snapping.

"Now, for mercy's sake, tell me what happened," she said, adding hotly, "and if I don't give that Maria Wendell a piece of my mind!"

Uncle Henry broke in: *"I'm* going to tell what happened. I *want* to do it. You and Mother just listen, just sit right down and listen." His voice was shaking with feeling, and as he went on and told of Betsy's afternoon, her fright, her confusion, her forming the plan of coming home on the train and of earning the money for the tickets, he made, for once, no Putney pretense of casual coolness. His old eyes flashed fire as he talked.

Betsy, watching him, felt her heart swell and beat fast in incredulous joy. Why, he was proud of her! She had done something to make the Putney cousins proud of her!

When Uncle Henry came to the part where she went on

asking for employment after one and then another refusal, Cousin Ann reached out her long arms and quickly, roughly, gathered Betsy up on her lap, holding her close as she listened. Betsy had never before sat on Cousin Ann's lap.

And when Uncle Henry finished—he had not forgotten a single thing Betsy had told him—and asked, "What do you think of *that* for a little girl ten years old today?" Cousin Ann opened the floodgates wide and burst out, "I think I never heard of a child's doing a smarter, grittier thing . . . *and I don't care if she does hear me say so!*"

It was a great, a momentous, an historic moment!

Betsy, enthroned on those strong knees, wondered if any little girl had ever had such a beautiful birthday.

"Understood
Aunt Frances"

About a month after Betsy's birthday, one October day when the leaves were all red and yellow, two very momentous events occurred, and, in a manner of speaking, at the very same time. Betsy had noticed that her kitten Eleanor (she still thought of her as a kitten, although she was now a big, grown-up cat) spent very little time around the house. She came into the kitchen two or three times a day, mewing loudly for milk and food, but after eating very fast she always disappeared at once. Betsy missed the purring, contented ball of fur on her lap in the long evenings as she played checkers, or read aloud, or sewed, or played guessing games. She felt rather hurt, too, that Eleanor paid her so little attention, and several times she tried hard to make her stay, trailing in front of her a spool tied to a string or rolling a worsted ball across the floor. But Eleanor seemed to have lost all her taste for the things she had liked so much. Invariably, the moment the door was opened, she darted out and vanished.

One afternoon Betsy ran out after her, determined to catch her and bring her back. When the cat found she was being followed, she bounded along in great leaps, constantly escaping from Betsy's outstretched hand. They came thus to the horse barn, into the open door of which Eleanor whisked like a little gray shadow, Betsy close behind. The cat flashed up the steep, ladderlike stairs that led to the hayloft. Betsy scrambled rapidly up, too. It was dark up there, compared to the gorgeous-colored October day outside, and for a moment she could not see Eleanor. Then she made her out, a dim little shape, picking her way over the hay, and she heard her talking. Yes, it was real talk, quite, quite different from the loud, imperious *"miauw!"* with which Eleanor asked for her milk. This was the softest, prettiest kind of conversation, all little murmurs and chirps and sing-songs. Why, Betsy could almost understand it! She *could* understand it enough to know that it was love talk, and then, breaking into this, came a sudden series of shrill, little, needlelike cries that fairly filled the hayloft. Eleanor gave a bound forward and disappeared. Betsy, very much excited, scrambled and climbed up over the hay as fast as she could go.

It was all silent now—the piercing, funny little squalls had stopped as suddenly as they began. On the top in a little nest lay Eleanor, purring so loudly you could hear her all over the big mow, and so proud and happy she could hardly contain herself. Her eyes glistened, she arched her back, rolled over and spread out her paws, disclosing to Betsy's astounded, delighted eyes—no, she wasn't dreaming

—two dear little kittens, one all gray, just like its mother; one gray with a big bib on his chest.

Oh! How dear they were! How darling, and cuddly, and fuzzy! Betsy put her fingers very softly on the gray one's head and thrilled to feel the warmth of the little living creature. "Oh, Eleanor!" she asked eagerly. "*Can* I pick one up?" She lifted the gray one gently and held it up to her cheek. The little thing nestled down in the warm hollow of her hand. She could feel its tiny, tiny little claws pricking softly into her palm. "Oh, you sweetness! You little, little babything!" she said over and over in a whisper.

Eleanor did not stop purring, and she looked up with friendly, trusting eyes as her little mistress made the acquaintance of her children, but Betsy could feel somehow that Eleanor was anxious about her kitten, was afraid that, although the little girl meant everything that was kind, her great, clumsy, awkward human hands weren't clever enough to hold a baby cat the proper way. "I don't blame you a bit, Eleanor," said Betsy. "I should feel just so in your place. There! I won't touch it again!" She laid the kitten down carefully by its mother. Eleanor at once began to wash its face vigorously, knocking it over and over with her strong tongue. "My!" said Betsy, laughing. "You'd scratch my eyes out, if *I* were as rough as that!"

Eleanor didn't seem to hear. Or rather she seemed to hear something else. For she stopped short, her head lifted, her ears pricked up, listening very hard to some distant sound. Then Betsy heard it, too, somebody coming into the barn below, little, quick, uneven footsteps. It must be little Molly, tagging along, as she always did. What fun to show Molly the kittens!

"Betsy!" called Molly from below.

"Molly!" called Betsy from above. "Come up here quick! I've got something up here."

There was a sound of scrambling, rapid feet on the rough stairs, and Molly's yellow curls appeared, shining in the dusk. "I've got a . . ." she began, but Betsy did not let her finish.

"Come here, Molly, quick! *quick!*" she called, beckoning eagerly, as though the kittens might evaporate into thin air if Molly didn't get there at once.

Molly forgot what she was going to say, climbed madly up the steep pile of hay, and in a moment was lying flat on her stomach beside the little family in a spasm of delight that satisfied even Betsy and Eleanor, both of them convinced that these were the finest kittens the world had ever seen.

"See, there are two," said Betsy. "You can have one for your very own. And I'll let you choose. Which one do you like best?"

She was hoping that Molly would not take the little all-gray one, because she had fallen in love with that the minute she saw it.

"Oh, *this* one with the white on his breast," said Molly, without a moment's hesitation. "It's *lots* the prettiest! Oh, Betsy! For my very own?"

Something white fell out of the folds of her skirt on the hay. "Oh, yes," she said indifferently. "A letter for you.

Miss Ann told me to bring it out here. She said she saw you streaking it for the barn."

It was a letter from Aunt Frances. Betsy opened it, one eye on Molly to see that she did not hug her new darling too tightly, and began to read it in the ray of dusty sunlight slanting through a crack in the side of the barn. She could do this easily, because Aunt Frances always made her handwriting very large and round and clear, so that a little girl could read it without half trying.

And as she read, everything faded away from before her . . . the barn, Molly, the kittens . . . she saw nothing but the words on the page.

When she had read the letter through she got up quickly, oh, ever so quickly! and went away down the stairs. Molly hardly noticed she had gone, so absorbing and delightful were the kittens.

Betsy went out of the dusky barn into the rich, October splendor and saw none of it. She went straight away from the house and the barn, straight up into the hill pasture toward her favorite place beside the brook, the shady pool under the big maple tree. At first she walked, but after a while she ran, faster and faster, as though she could not get there soon enough. Her head was down, and one arm was crooked over her face. . . .

And do you know, I'm not going to follow her up there, nor let you go. I'm afraid we would all cry if we saw what Betsy did under the big maple tree. The reason she ran away so fast was so that she could be all by herself for a very hard hour, and fight it out, alone.

So let us go back soberly to the orchard where the

Putneys are, and wait till Betsy comes walking listlessly in, her eyes red and her cheeks pale. Cousin Ann was up in the top of a tree, a basket hung over her shoulder half full of striped red Northern Spies; Uncle Henry was on a ladder against another tree, filling a bag with the beautiful, shining, yellow-green Pound Sweets, and Aunt Abigail was moving around, picking up the parti-colored windfalls and putting them into barrels ready to go to the cider mill.

Something about the way Betsy walked, and as she drew closer something about the expression of her face, and oh! as she began to speak, something about the tone of her voice, stopped all this cheerful activity as though a bomb had gone off in their midst.

"I've had a letter from Aunt Frances," said Betsy. "She says she's coming to take me away, back to them, tomorrow."

There was a big silence; Cousin Ann stood, perfectly motionless up in her tree, staring down through the leaves at Betsy. Uncle Henry was turned around on his ladder, one hand on an apple as though it had frozen there, staring down at Betsy. Aunt Abigail leaned with both fat hands on her barrel, staring hard at Betsy. Betsy was staring down at her shoes, biting her lips and winking her eyes. The yellow, hazy October sun sank slowly down toward the rim of Hemlock Mountain, and sent long, golden shafts of light through the branches of the trees upon this group of people, all so silent, so motionless.

Betsy was the first to speak, and I'm proud of her for what she said. She said, loyally, "Dear Aunt Frances! She was always so sweet to me! She always tried so hard to take care of me!"

For that was what Betsy had found up by the brook under the big red maple tree. She had found there a certainty that, whatever else she did, she must *not* hurt Aunt Frances's feelings—dear, gentle, sweet Aunt Frances, whose feelings were so easily hurt and who had given her so many years of such anxious care. Something up there had told her—perhaps the quiet blue shadow of Windward Mountain creeping slowly over the pasture toward her, perhaps the silent glory of the red and gold tree, perhaps the singing murmur of the little brook—perhaps all of them together had told her that now had come a time when she must do more than what Cousin Ann would do—when she must do what she herself knew was right. And that was to protect Aunt Frances from hurt.

When she spoke, out there in the orchard, she broke the spell of silence. Cousin Ann climbed hastily down from her tree, with her basket only partly filled. Uncle Henry got stiffly off his ladder, and Aunt Abigail advanced through the grass. And they all said the same thing—"Let me see that letter."

They read it there, looking over each other's shoulders, with grave faces. Then, still silently, they all turned and went back into the house, leaving their forgotten bags and barrels and baskets out under the trees. When they found themselves in the kitchen—"Well, it's suppertime, anyhow," said Cousin Ann hastily, as if ashamed of losing her composure, "or almost time. We might as well get it now."

"I'm a-going out to milk," said Uncle Henry gruffly, although it was not nearly his usual time. He took up the milk pails and marched out toward the barn, stepping heavily, his head hanging.

Shep woke up with a snort and, getting off the couch, gamboled clumsily up to Betsy, wagging his tail and jumping up on her, ready for a frolic. That was almost too much for Betsy! To think that after tomorrow she would never see Shep again—nor Eleanor! Nor the kittens! She choked as she bent over Shep and put her arms around his neck for a great hug. But she mustn't cry, she mustn't hurt Aunt Frances's feelings, or show that she wasn't glad to go back to her. That wouldn't be fair, after all Aunt Frances had done for her!

That night she lay awake after she and Molly had gone to bed and Molly was asleep. They had decided not to tell Molly until the last minute, so she had dropped off peacefully, as usual. But poor Betsy's eyes were wide open. She saw a gleam of light under the door. It widened; the door opened. Aunt Abigail stood there, in her night cap, mountainous in her long white gown, a candle shining up into her serious old face.

"You awake, Betsy?" she whispered, seeing the child's dark eyes gleaming at her over the covers. "I just—I just thought I'd look in to see if you were all right." She came to the edge of the bed and set the candle down on the little stand. Betsy reached her arms up longingly and the old woman stooped over her. Neither of them said a single word during the long embrace which followed. Then Aunt Abigail straightened up hastily, took her candle quickly and softly, and heavily padded out of the room.

Betsy turned over and flung one arm over Molly—no Molly, either, after tomorrow!

She gulped hard and stared up at the ceiling, dimly white in the starlight. A gleam of light shone under the door. It widened, and Uncle Henry stood there, a candle in his hand, peering into the room. "You awake, Betsy?" he said cautiously.

"Yes. I'm awake, Uncle Henry."

The old man shuffled into the room. "I just got to thinking," he said, hesitating, "that maybe you'd like to take my watch with you. It's kind of handy to have a watch on the train. And I'd like real well for you to have it."

He laid it down on the stand, his own cherished gold watch, that had been given him when he was twenty-one.

Betsy reached out and took his hard, gnarled old fist in a tight grip. "Oh, Uncle Henry!" she began, and could not go on.

"We'll miss you, Betsy," he said in an uncertain voice. "It's been . . . it's been real nice to have you here . . ."

And then he too snatched up his candle very quickly and almost ran out of the room.

Betsy turned over on her back. "No crying now!" she told herself fiercely. "No crying now!" She clenched her hands together tightly and set her teeth.

Something moved in the room. Somebody leaned over her. It was Cousin Ann, who didn't make a sound, not one, but who took Betsy in her strong arms and held her close and closer, till Betsy could feel the quick pulse of the other's heart beating all through her own body.

Then she was gone—as silently as she came.

But somehow that great embrace had taken away all the burning tightness from Betsy's eyes and heart. She was very tired, and soon after this she fell asleep, snuggled up close to Molly.

In the morning, nobody spoke of last night. Breakfast was prepared and eaten, and the team hitched up directly afterward. Betsy and Uncle Henry were to drive to the station together to meet Aunt Frances's train. Betsy put on her new wine-colored cashmere that Cousin Ann had made her, with the soft white collar of delicate old embroidery that Aunt Abigail had given her out of one of the trunks in the attic.

She and Uncle Henry said little as they drove to the village, and even less as they stood waiting together on the platform. Betsy slipped her hand into his and he held it tight as the train whistled in the distance and came slowly and laboriously puffing up to the station.

Just one person got off at the little station, and that was Aunt Frances, looking dressed up and citified, with kid gloves and a white veil over her face and a big blue one floating from her gay-flowered velvet hat. How pretty she was! And how young—under the veil which hid so kindly the little lines in her sweet, thin face. And how excited and fluttery! Betsy had forgotten how fluttery Aunt Frances was! She clasped Betsy to her, and then started back crying —she must see to her satchel—and then she clasped Betsy to her again and shook hands with Uncle Henry, whose grim old face looked about as cordial and welcoming as the sourest kind of sour pickle, and she fluttered back and said she must have left her umbrella on the train. "Oh, Conductor! Conductor! My umbrella—right in my seat—a blue one with a crooked-over—oh, here it is in my hand! What am I thinking of!"

The conductor evidently thought he'd better get the train away as soon as possible, for he now shouted, "All aboard!" to nobody at all, and sprang back on the steps. The train went off, groaning over the steep grade, and screaming out its usual echoing warning about the next road crossing.

Uncle Henry took Aunt Frances's satchel and plodded back to the surrey. He got into the front seat and Aunt Frances and Betsy in the back; and they started off.

Now I want you to listen to every single word that was said on the back seat, for it was a very important conversation, when Betsy's fate hung on the curl of an eyelash and the flicker of a voice, as fates often do.

Aunt Frances hugged Betsy again and again and exclaimed about her having grown so big and tall and fat— she didn't say brown too, although you could see that she was thinking that, as she looked through her veil at Betsy's tanned face and down at the contrast between her own pretty, white fingers and Betsy's leather-colored, muscular little hands. She exclaimed and exclaimed and kept on exclaiming! Betsy wondered if she really always had been as fluttery as this. Then, all of a sudden it came out, the great news, the reason for the extra flutteriness.

Aunt Frances was going to be married!

Yes! Think of it! Betsy fell back open-mouthed with astonishment.

Did Betsy think her Aunt Frances a silly old thing?

"Oh, Aunt Frances, *no!*" cried Betsy fervently. "You look just as *young*, and pretty! Lots younger than I remembered you!"

Aunt Frances flushed with pleasure and went on, "You'll love your old Aunt Frances just as much, won't you, when she's Mrs. Plimpton?"

Betsy put her arms around her and gave her a great hug. "I'll always love you, Aunt Frances!" she said.

"You'll love Mr. Plimpton, too. He's so big and strong, and he just loves to take care of people. He says that's why he's marrying me. Don't you wonder where we are going to live?" she asked, answering her own question quickly. "We're not going to live anywhere. Isn't that a joke? Mr. Plimpton's business keeps him always moving around from one place to another, never more than a month anywhere."

"What'll Aunt Harriet do?" asked Betsy wonderingly.

"Why, she's ever and ever so much better," said Aunt Frances happily. "And her own sister, my Aunt Rachel, has come back from China, where she's been a missionary for ever so long, and the two old ladies are going to keep house together out in California, in the dearest little bungalow, all roses and honeysuckle. But *you're* going to be with me. Won't it be jolly fun, darling, to go traveling all about everywhere, and see new places all the time?"

Now those are the words Aunt Frances said, but something in her voice and her face suggested a faint possibility to Betsy that maybe Aunt Frances didn't really think it would be such awfully jolly fun as her words said.

Her heart gave a big jump up, and she had to hold tight to the arm of the surrey before she could ask, in a quiet voice, "But, Aunt Frances, won't I be awfully in your way, traveling around so?"

Now, Aunt Frances had ears of her own, and though that was what Betsy's words said, what Aunt Frances heard was a suggestion that possibly Betsy wasn't as crazy to leave Putney Farm as she had supposed of course she would be.

They both stopped talking for a moment and peered at each other through the thicket of words that held them apart. I told you this was a very momentous conversation. One sure thing is that the people on the back seat saw the inside of the surrey as they traveled along, and nothing else. Red sumac and bronzed beech trees waved their flags at them in vain. They kept their eyes fixed on each other intently, each in an agony of fear lest she hurt the other's feelings.

After a pause Aunt Frances came to herself with a start, and said, affectionately putting her arm around Betsy, "Why, you darling, what does Aunt Frances care about trouble if her own dear baby girl is happy?"

And Betsy said, resolutely, "Oh, you know, Aunt Frances, I'd *love* to be with you!" She ventured one more step through the thicket. "But honestly, Aunt Frances, *won't* it be a bother? . . ."

Aunt Frances ventured another step to meet her, "But dear little girls must be *somewhere* . . ."

And Betsy almost forgot her caution and burst out, "But I could stay here! I know they would keep me!"

Even Aunt Frances's two veils could not hide the gleam

of relief and hope that came into her pretty, thin, sweet face. She summoned all her courage and stepped out into the clearing in the middle of the thicket, asking right out, boldly, "Why, do you like it here, Betsy? Would you like to stay?"

And Betsy—she never could remember afterward if she had been careful enough not to shout too loudly and joy-fully—Betsy cried out, "Oh, I *love* it here!" There they stood, face-to-face, looking at each other with honest and very happy eyes.

Aunt Frances threw her arm around Betsy and asked again, "Are you *sure*, dear?" and didn't try to hide her relief. And neither did Betsy.

"I could visit you once in a while, when you are some-where near here," suggested Betsy, beaming.

"Oh, *yes*, I must have *some* of the time with my darling!" said Aunt Frances. And this time there was nothing in their hearts that contradicted their lips.

They clung to each other as Uncle Henry guided the surrey up to the marble stepping-stone. Betsy jumped out first, and while Uncle Henry was helping Aunt Frances out, she was dashing up the walk like a crazy thing. She flung open the front door and catapulted into Aunt Abigail just coming out. It was like flinging herself into a feather-bed. . . .

"Oh! Oh!" she gasped out. "Aunt Frances is going to be married. And travel around all the time! And she doesn't *really* want me at all! Can't I stay here? Can't I stay here?"

Cousin Ann was right behind Aunt Abigail, and she heard this. She looked over their shoulders toward Aunt

Frances, who was approaching from behind, and said, in her usual calm and collected voice: "How do you do, Frances? Glad to see you, Frances. How well you're looking! I hear you are in for congratulations. Who's the happy man?"

Betsy was overcome with admiration for her coolness in being able to talk so in such an exciting moment. She knew Aunt Abigail couldn't have done it, for she had sat down in a rocking chair, and was holding Betsy on her lap. The little girl could see her wrinkled old hand trembling on the arm of the chair.

"I hope that means," continued Cousin Ann, going as usual straight to the point, "that we can keep Betsy here with us."

"Oh, would you like to?" asked Aunt Frances, fluttering, as though the idea had never occurred to her before that minute. "Would Elizabeth Ann really *like* to stay?"

"Oh, I'd *like* to, all right!" said Betsy, looking confidently up into Aunt Abigail's face.

Aunt Abigail spoke now. She cleared her throat twice before she could bring out a word. Then she said, "Why, yes, we'd kind of like to keep her. We've sort of got used to having her around."

That's what she *said*, but, as you have noticed before on this exciting day, what people said didn't matter as much as what they looked; and as her old lips pronounced these words so quietly, the corners of Aunt Abigail's mouth were twitching, and she was swallowing hard. She said, impatiently, to Cousin Ann, "Hand me that handkerchief,

Ann!" And as she blew her nose, she said, "What an old fool I am!"

It was as though a great, fresh breeze had blown through the house. They all drew a long breath and began to talk loudly and cheerfully about the weather and Aunt Frances's trip and how Aunt Harriet was and which room Aunt Frances was to have and would she leave her wraps down in the hall or take them upstairs—and, in the midst of this, Betsy, her heart ready to burst, dashed out of doors, followed by Shep. She ran madly toward the barn. She did not know where she was going. She only knew that she must run and jump and shout, or she would explode.

Shep ran and jumped because Betsy did.

To these two wild creatures, careering through the air like bright blown autumn leaves, appeared little Molly in the barn door.

"Oh, I'm going to stay! I'm going to stay!" screamed Betsy.

But as Molly had not had any notion of the contrary, she only said, "Of course, why not?" and went on to something important, saying, "My kitten can *walk!* It took *three steps* just now."

After Aunt Frances got her wraps off, Betsy took her for a tour of inspection. They went all over the house first, with special emphasis laid on the kitchen-living room. "Isn't this the loveliest place?" said Betsy, fervently, looking about her at the white curtains, the bright flowers, the southern sunshine, the bookcases, and the bright cooking utensils. It was all full to the brim to her eyes with happiness. She forgot entirely that she had thought it a very poor, common kind of room when she had first seen it. Nor did she notice that Aunt Frances showed no enthusiasm over it now.

She stopped for a few moments to wash some potatoes and put them into the oven for dinner. Aunt Frances opened her eyes at this. "I always see to the potatoes and the apples, the cooking of them, I mean," explained Betsy proudly. "I've just learned to make apple pie and brown betty."

Then down into the stone-floored milkroom, where Aunt Abigail was working over butter, and where Betsy, swelling with pride, showed Aunt Frances how deftly and smoothly she could manipulate the wooden paddle and make rolls of butter that weighed within an ounce or two of a pound.

"Mercy, child! Think of your being able to do such things!" said Aunt Frances, more and more astonished.

They went out of doors now, Shep bounding by their side. Betsy was amazed to see that Aunt Frances drew back, nervously, whenever the big dog frisked near her. Out in the barn Betsy had a disappointment. Aunt Frances just balked absolutely at those ladderlike stairs—"Oh, I *couldn't*! I couldn't, dear. Do *you* go up there? Is it quite safe?"

"Why, *Aunt Abigail* went up there to see the kittens!" cried Betsy, on the edge of exasperation. But her heart softened at the sight of Aunt Frances's evident distress of mind at the idea of climbing into the loft, and she brought the kittens down for inspection, Eleanor mewing anxiously at the top of the stairs.

On the way back to the house they had an adventure, a sort of adventure, and it brought home to Betsy once for all how much she loved dear, sweet Aunt Frances, and what kind of love it was.

As they crossed the barnyard the calf approached them playfully, leaping stiff-legged into the air, and making a pretense of butting at them with its hornless young head.

Betsy and Shep often played with the calf in this way by the half hour, and she thought nothing of it now; hardly noticed it, in fact.

But Aunt Frances gave a loud, piercing shriek, as though she were being cut into pieces. "Help! *Help!*" she screamed. "Betsy! Oh, Betsy!"

She had turned white and could not take a single step forward. "It's nothing! It's nothing!" said Betsy, rather impatiently. "He's just playing. We often play with him, Shep and I."

The calf came a little nearer, with lowered head. *"Get* away!" said Betsy indifferently, kicking at him.

At this hint of masterfulness on Betsy's part, Aunt Frances cried out, "Oh, yes, Betsy, *do* make him go away! Do make him go away!"

It came over Betsy that Aunt Frances was frightened, yes, really; and all at once her impatience disappeared, never to come back again. She felt toward Aunt Frances just as she did toward little Molly, and she acted accordingly. She stepped in front of Aunt Frances, picked up a stick, and hit the calf a blow on the neck with it. He moved away, startled and injured, looking at his playfellow with reproachful eyes. But Betsy was relentless. Aunt Frances must not be frightened!

"Here, Shep! Here, Shep!" she called loudly, and when the big dog came bounding to her she pointed to the calf and said sternly, "Take him into the barn! Drive him into the barn, sir!"

Shep asked nothing better than this command, and charged forward, barking furiously and leaping into the air as though he intended to eat the calf up alive. The two swept across the barnyard and into the lower regions of the barn. In a moment Shep reappeared, his tongue hanging out, his tail wagging, his eyes glistening, very proud of himself, and mounted guard at the door.

Aunt Frances hurried along through the gate of the barnyard. As it fell to behind her she sank down on a rock, breathless, still pale and agitated. Betsy threw her arms around her in a transport of affection. She felt that she *understood* Aunt Frances as nobody else could, the dear, sweet, gentle, timid aunt! She took the thin, nervous white fingers in her strong brown hands. "Oh, Aunt Frances, darling Aunt Frances!" she cried. "How I wish I could *always* take care of you."

The last of the red and gold leaves were slowly drifting to the ground as Betsy and Uncle Henry drove back from the station after seeing Aunt Frances off. They were not silent this time, as when they had gone to meet her. They were talking cheerfully together, laying their plans for the winter which was so near. "I must begin to bank the house tomorrow," mused Uncle Henry. "And those apples have got to go to the cider mill, right off. Don't you want to ride over on top of them, Betsy, and see 'em made into cider?"

"Oh, my, yes!" said Betsy. "That will be fine! And I must put away Deborah's summer clothes and get Cousin Ann to help me make some warm ones, if I'm going to take her to school in cold weather."

As they drove into the yard, they saw Eleanor coming from the direction of the barn with something big and heavy in her mouth. She held her head as high as she could, but even so, her burden dragged on the ground, bumping softly against the rough places on the path. "Look!" said Betsy. "Just see that great rat Eleanor has caught!"

Uncle Henry squinted his old eyes toward the cat for a moment and laughed. "We're not the only ones that are getting ready for winter," he remarked.

Betsy did not know what he meant and climbed hastily over the wheel and ran to see. As she approached Eleanor, the cat laid her burden down with an air of relief and looked trustfully into her little mistress's face. Why, it was one of the kittens! Eleanor was bringing it to the house. Oh, of course! They mustn't stay out there in that cold hayloft now the cold weather was drawing near. Betsy picked up the little sprawling thing, trying with weak legs to get around over the rough ground. She carried it carefully toward the house, Eleanor walking sinuously by her side and "talking" in little singing, purring *miauws* to explain her ideas of kitten comfort. Betsy felt that she quite understood her. "Yes, Eleanor, a nice little basket behind the stove with a warm piece of an old blanket in it. Yes, I'll fix it for you. It'll be lovely to have the whole family there. And I'll bring the other one in for you."

But evidently Eleanor did not understand little-girl talk as well as Betsy understood cat talk, for a little later, as Betsy turned from the nest she was making in the corner behind the stove, Eleanor was missing; and when she ran out toward the barn she met her again, her head strained painfully back, dragging another fat, heavy kitten, who curled his pink feet up as high as he could in a vain effort not to have them knock against the stones. "Now, Eleanor," said Betsy, a little put out, "you don't trust me enough! I was going to get it all right!"

"Well," said Aunt Abigail, as they came into the kitchen, "now you must begin to teach them to drink."

"Goodness!" said Betsy. "Don't they know how to drink already?"

"You try them and see," said Aunt Abigail with a mysterious smile.

So when Uncle Henry brought the pails full of fragrant, warm milk into the house, Betsy poured out some in a saucer and put the kittens up to it. She and Molly squatted down on their heels to watch, and before long they were laughing so that they were rolling on the kitchen floor. At first the kittens looked every way but at the milk, seeming to see everything but what was under their noses. Then Graykin (that was Betsy's) absentmindedly walked right through the saucer, emerging with very wet feet and an aggrieved and astonished expression. Molly screamed with laughter to see him shake his pink toes and sit down seriously to lick them clean. Then White-bib (Molly's) put his head down to the saucer.

"There! Mine is smarter than yours!" said Molly. But White-bib went on putting his head down, down, down, clear into the milk nearly up to his eyes, although he looked frightened and miserable. Then he jerked it up quickly and sneezed and sneezed and sneezed, such deliciously funny little baby sneezes! He pawed and pawed at his little pink nose with his little pink paw until Eleanor took pity on him and came to wash him off. In the midst of this process she saw the milk, and left off to lap it up eagerly; and in a jiffy she had drunk every drop and was licking the saucer loudly with her raspy tongue. That was the end of the kittens' first lesson.

In the evening, as they sat around the lamp, Eleanor came and got up in Betsy's lap just like old times. Betsy was playing checkers with Uncle Henry and interrupted the game to welcome the cat back. But Eleanor was uneasy, and kept stopping her toilet to prick up her ears and look restlessly toward the basket, where the kittens lay curled so closely together that they looked like one soft ball of gray fur. By and by Eleanor jumped down heavily and went back to the basket. She stayed there only a moment, standing over the kittens and licking them. The she came back and got up in Betsy's lap again.

"What ails that cat?" said Cousin Ann, noting this pacing and restlessness.

"Maybe she wants Betsy to hold her kittens, too," suggested Aunt Abigail.

"Oh, I'd love to!" said Betsy, spreading out her knees to make her lap bigger.

"But I want my own White-bib myself!" said Molly, looking up from the beads she was stringing.

"Well, maybe Eleanor would let you settle it that way," said Cousin Ann.

The little girls ran over to the basket and brought back each her own kitten. Eleanor watched them anxiously, but as soon as they sat down she jumped up happily into Betsy's lap and curled down close to Graykin. This time she was completely satisfied, and her loud purring filled the room with a peaceable murmur.

"There, now you're fixed for the winter," said Aunt Abigail.

By and by, after Cousin Ann had popped some corn, old Shep got off the couch and came to stand by Betsy's knee to get an occasional handful. Eleanor opened one eye, recognized a friend, and shut it sleepily. But the kitten woke up in terrible alarm to see that hideous monster so near him, and prepared to sell his life dearly. He bristled up his ridiculous short tail, opened his absurd, pink mouth in a soft, baby s—s—s, and struck savagely at old Shep's good-natured face with a soft little paw. Betsy felt her heart overflow with amusement and pride in the intrepid little morsel. She burst into laughter, but she picked it up and held it lovingly close to her cheek. What fun it was going to be to see those kittens grow up!

Old Shep padded back softly to the couch, his toenails clicking on the floor, hoisted himself heavily up, and went to sleep. The kitten subsided into a ball again. Eleanor stirred and stretched in her sleep and laid her head in utter trust on her little mistress's hand. After that Betsy moved the checkers only with her other hand.

In the intervals of the game, while Uncle Henry was pondering over his moves, the little girl looked down at her pets and listened absently to the keen autumnal wind that swept around the old house, shaking the shutters and rattling the windows. A stick of wood in the stove burned in two and fell together with a soft, whispering sound. The lamp cast a steady radiance on Uncle Henry bent seriously over the checkerboard, on Molly's blooming, round cheeks and bright hair, on Aunt Abigail's rosy, cheerful, wrinkled old face, and on Cousin Ann's quiet, clear, dark eyes. . . .

That room was full to the brim of something beautiful, and Betsy knew what it was. Its name was Happiness.

Afterword

Peggy Parish

Over the years many books have become my friends. Among my most favorite is *Understood Betsy*. I don't remember when I first met Betsy. She has been around even longer than I have. But every few years I take that book off the shelf and settle down for a good read. Although I have grown older and Betsy hasn't, I still laugh and get teary at the same places in the story. It's reassuring to find that some things don't change.

You may say it's old-fashioned, and it is, but it reflects the way it was in the early 1900s when the story was written. It presents a good picture of the progress made in just a few decades.

Yes, the author does intrude to question the reader and make comments. This does interrupt the story. Just skip those parts.

In the first chapter Elizabeth Ann is a real wimp. But how could she help but be? The only thing she is allowed to do for herself is breathe, and I'm sure Aunt Frances would do that for her if she could. Poor Elizabeth Ann doesn't know a thing about the real world. Yet she does show a glimmer of spark when she tells Aunt Frances her dreams and adds all kinds of awful things.

What a horrendous experience for Elizabeth Ann to be thrust from the nest and sent to those "awful Putneys." Can't you imagine how frightened she was? I'm sure that at age nine I, too, would have been frightened.

To me, Elizabeth Ann began to show true grit during her ride to the farm with Uncle Henry. Suddenly this overprotected little girl is given the reins and told to drive those huge horses. Like many of us, she had trouble with left and right. In puzzling through this problem, something clicked in her mind. All she had to do was pull the way she wanted the horses to go. Right and left made no difference. What an exciting discovery!

I took an instant liking to Cousin Ann. I was delighted when she would have no part of the formal-sounding "Elizabeth Ann" and opted to call the child by the down-to-earth name of Betsy. I was surprised that Elizabeth Ann had no reaction to being called Betsy. Wouldn't you have made some comment if your name was changed?

Wasn't it nice the way Aunt Abigail handled things when she realized Betsy was feeling homesick? Rather than cuddle and sympathize with her, which would have made matters worse, she plopped a kitten on her lap. How could Aunt Abigail have known that Betsy had always wanted a kitten? Or did she just know that kittens and children go together?

In several places in the story we are given indications that Betsy has been taught that people of her kind are above domestic work. When Cousin Ann suggests that

Betsy wash her dishes, we are told, "Elizabeth Ann had never washed a dish in all her life, and she had always thought that nobody but poor, ignorant people, who couldn't afford to hire girls, did such things." This attitude was quite prevalent at that time, though I must admit I could never see what being poor and ignorant had to do with washing dishes. My family was neither poor nor ignorant, but washing dishes was one of my chores from an early age.

In many ways Betsy is no different from you. It's the circumstances that differ. You may never find yourself having the experiences that Betsy had. Have you ever churned butter? When Betsy was helping make butter, we are told, "She weighed out the salt needed on the scales, and was very much surprised to find that there really is such a thing as an ounce. She had never met it before outside the pages of her arithmetic book and she didn't know it lived anywhere else." Have you ever met an ounce face-to-face? Do you know how an ounce of something looks or how heavy it feels? Not many of us do.

Aunt Frances always told people how delicate Betsy's digestion was and that she ate only enough to keep a bird alive. Poor Betsy thought she must live up to this. But the Putneys don't seem to have this information, so Betsy happily forgets it. She eats so much, she feels her belt grow tight, a new experience for her.

What a giant hurdle it must have been for Betsy to get herself to a new school where she knew no one. But I must admit I envy Betsy's getting to go to a one-room school. They were around when I was a child, but we lived in town and I had to go to a regular school. Wouldn't it be fun to be in different grades for different subjects? What a lift it must have given Betsy to be asked to read with little Molly. To be able to help someone else was certainly a new experience, and one I think she liked.

One of the most exciting discoveries for Betsy was made that first day of school. The story tells us, "She had always thought she was there to pass from one grade to another, and she was ever so startled to get a glimpse of the fact that she was there to learn how to read and write and cipher and generally use her mind, so she could take care of herself when she came to be grown up."

It's fun to watch Betsy become one of the gang—gossiping with the girls, having friends over to play, and initiating such projects as making new clothes for poor little 'Lias.

How wise Betsy is in choosing Cousin Ann as a role model and in trying to think like Cousin Ann in order to rescue little Molly from the pit.

What courage Betsy shows when she and Molly are stranded at the fair. Although she is afraid, she does what has to be done to get herself and Molly home. That's what courage is all about.

In many ways, Dorothy Canfield Fisher is ahead of her time. Did you notice Betsy was never told, "Girls don't do that," or "You must act like a young lady"? Nor was she told, "You mustn't feel that way," or "You can't do that." She was accepted and treated as an equal member of the family. Did you notice there was no division between men and women's work? Uncle Henry helped with the butter making and Cousin Ann was into everything. I doubt this family would have any difficulty in adapting to present times. Cousin Ann would probably climb to the top of the corporate ladder very quickly.

In a few years I expect I'll once again take this book from the shelf and have myself a good read. I hope you will want to do the same.